"I DIDN'T KILL HIM," I SAID

I don't know how long I stood there. All the past came swirling up around me, making everything I saw unreal. It can't be, I found my mind saying, it can't be.

But it was. There on the couch was the body, and there was the knife I had made for my brother fifteen years before. I made it from a handful of pesos and a needle-sharp piece of stone—a bit of obsidian that I had found near the Temple of Quetzalcoatl. Arthur had said it was a sacrificial knife centuries ago. I had made the hilt of silver dollars and had fitted it on the stone shaft. If you twisted it a certain way, the blade and the hilt parted, and in the space inside I had carefully engraved my brother's name. At the time that had seemed very appealing—like a secret passageway or an undiscovered drawer in an old desk.

Mitchell Drake had come back to Mexico City to find his missing brother, Arthur. Instead, he found the knife . . . the knife with the name inside, left behind like a calling card . . . the knife for whose treasured secret, murder had just been done . . . the knife that was still warm with the blood of an old friend.

About THE COVER

In old Mexico, where life is cheap, and treasure is fabled, the silver-handled knife held a deadly secret. The strong arm that grasped it sought a glittering treasure hoard. The unwary back beneath it found only sudden death.

Illustrated by Bob Doares.

The Case of the Mexican Knife

Originally published under the title
The Street of the Crying Woman

By

GEOFFREY HOMES

BANTAM BOOKS
NEW YORK

A BANTAM BOOK *published by arrangement with*
William Morrow and Company, Inc.

Bantam Edition Published
November 1948

Originally published under the title
The Street of the Crying Woman

Copyright, 1942, by William Morrow and Company, Inc.

 Bantam Books are published by Bantam Books, Inc. Its trade mark, consisting of the words "BANTAM BOOKS" and the portrayal of a bantam as here reproduced, is registered in the U. S. Patent Office.

Printed in the United States of America

To
Kelly Browne
And
Mitchell Rawson

CAST OF CHARACTERS

MITCHELL DRAKE was an instructor in a New England school . . . until his brother, Arthur, disappeared in Mexico.

PENNY GAGE was a pupil of Mitchell's . . . but not too young to teach him a few things about life.

MOLLY GAGE, her aunt, was a devastatingly logical woman.

JACQUES MAGNIN was a best-selling author.

PAUL BRENT had the face of an angel.

JOHN ALDRICH had been the Drakes' attorney in Mexico City for many years.

JOE BRIGGS was a newspaperman, an old friend of the Drakes.

DOROTHY ALLEN was Arthur's fiancée . . . a dancer, blonde, and very lovely.

RUIZ and **AMARO** had known Arthur before he disappeared.

JOSÉ MANUEL MADERO was an expert at knitting.

ONE

SOME DAY I'll go back to Mexico again. I'll take the long straight road south from Laredo, down through the jungle to Tamazanchale, then up and up over the hills to the broad valley where the manguey plants march across the plain in gray-green rows. Off to the left I'll see the White Woman sleeping in the mist, and beyond, the white cone of the Smoking Mountain. There will be organ cactus sheltering the little huts. There will be men and women and children trudging along the roads carrying their incredible loads. There will be dust and sun and wind and in a field a herd of white goats grazing.

Oh, I know it well, for I was born there. I know the feel of it and the smell of it and the warmth of it. I know its many voices.

Some day I'll walk along the narrow pitted pavements of Mexico City again, past the Alameda, past the House of the Blue Tiles, across the Zocalo and around the palace to the crowded markets. Kids will pull at my coat and ask softly for just one little penny. Old women will thrust lottery tickets in front of me, their dark eyes begging me to buy. I'll see a squat, serape-wrapped man knitting a sock as he shuffles along. And out toward San Angel I'll come upon a man and a fat pig he is taking to market sleeping in the shade of a pepper tree.

I'll take the road across the range and from the cliffs back of Tepozitlan I'll watch the thunderstorms sweep up the narrow valley. And I'll follow the winding road south, see the red tile roofs of Taxco, hear the ringing of the hammers of the silversmiths, then south through the cane fields and melon fields, down through the canyons and up a little hill, and once again I'll see the blue crescent that is the Bay of Acapulco.

Yes, I'll go back again. Not for a while, not until some of the wounds are healed, not until time puts its dream-like quality on the past, not until I forget—if that is possible—those days of terror and confusion and sudden death.

* * *

It started with a letter. I found it on my desk one morning early in October, a chill, drear morning with no sun. The handwriting on the envelope told me it was from my brother. I didn't open it at once. The postmark and the stamp brought the past rushing back. I remembered a city sleeping in the sun. I remembered dusty roads and desert and mountains shouldering the clouds aside. I remembered bright colors and soft voices and someone singing in the darkness.

I stood at the window, the letter in my hand, and there was another world outside, the hot, bright world of my youth. I saw again the hacienda on the hill back of San Angel. I ran through the cool halls out into the sun-filled patio where my mother was waiting for me. My brother Arthur was stretched out on the warm stones staring at the sky.

"If you brush my hair I'll read to you," Mother said.

Her bright hair swept down over her shoulders almost to her waist. I took the brush from her and went to work.

"Gently, Mitchell," Mother said.

"He thinks he's currying the horse," Arthur said.

"Why don't you do it then?" I said.

"It's your turn," Arthur said.

She opened the book and started to read, her voice as soft as the mass of hair under my hand. I stood there brushing her hair with long, even strokes, while she read *The Princess and the Goblin,* and after a while I stopped brushing and just listened.

That bright world faded. The sun was gone. There were slate-colored clouds low over the Westchester hills and a cold wind blowing. Good days, I thought, much too good to last. I pushed the past away, turned back to my littered desk and tore the envelope open. The letter was on the stationary of the Mexican Bureau of Anthropology in Guadalajara, and he had written:

Dear Mitch,

Today I handed my resignation to Don Alfonso. No, I didn't tell him off, though I wanted to. What good would it have done—he's too stupid to realize what a mess he has made of this office. Anyway, I think he intended to sack me and put one of his innumerable relatives in my place. That's what he has been doing ever since Dr. Guittierez backed the wrong political horse and found Don Alfonso in his chair. Ruiz, Ramirez, Orozco and Amaro—the guys I lived with so long—and all the other good men have had the can tied to them. My name should have been next on the list.

But don't worry about me. There is something in the wind, something so big I can say nothing about it. You know how it is when you talk too much about a thing, dream too much about it. It doesn't pan out. All I can tell you is this—if things go well we'll be rich and you can quit that silly job and go traipsing off with me. We'll go south to Chile and across the Andes and up to Rio, maybe. We'll do all the things we've wanted to do so long. (Unless, of course, the world goes thoroughly to pot, which it seems to be doing with remarkable speed.)

I'm all packed and waiting for the train, which won't be more than three hours late. Yes, the train service is just the same as it always was. Until you hear from me again my address will be care of John Aldrich, Av. Madero 86, Mexico, D.F. I plan to lease a house and there will be a room for you if you want to forget that precious sense of honor and consider me paid off. Maybe next summer, huh?

Take care of yourself and keep out of the clutches of your young charges. By the way, the job you did on Zapata was a good one. It made me proud my name was Drake. Or did I tell you that before? Love.

Arthur

I put the letter aside, feeling faintly guilty. It had been weeks since I had thought about Arthur, since I had thought about anything really but my own narrow life and my own petty problems. I hadn't forgotten him though. I couldn't do that.

We were born in Mexico City, Arthur and I. He preceded me into the world by five years and from the first he loved me. Mother said she expected him to be jealous when she brought me home. But he wasn't.

I don't remember much about those first few years. I remember a burro we had called Pancho, and Dolores, the Indian woman, who took care of us. I remember the trail that led from the hills past our house, down which came the donkey caravans laden with firewood. I remember the glow of the charcoal-makers' fires up in the mountains late at night and the good smell of smoke. I remember Father coming home from his long trips south and how good it was to see him.

Father was a mining engineer for the Mexican government and a good deal of the time he was off somewhere. Once in a while we went with him. He loaded us into an old seven-passenger Reo and we climbed the bumpy road over the mountains to Cuernavaca, a day's journey then. And it was another day's trip to Taxco where the silver mines were. Once, I remember, we made a pack trip far back into the hills to some little town that had been forgotten for centuries and we camped beside a creek and played with little boys who couldn't understand Mexican, who talked a strange language I had never heard.

But it is Mexico City and San Angel that I remember most. We went to a Catholic school in San Angel for a while. Later on, we moved to a house near the bull ring in Mexico City because Mother wanted us to be around children who spoke English. It was a fine life. And I'd be there yet probably if Father and Mother hadn't gone to Acapulco in June of 1927.

I suppose time is a good thing. After a while you can look back without too much pain. That morning there was a letter from Mother. They had a little place on the cliff where the

El Mirador hotel is now, and every day they walked down into the town and through it to the beach. Sometimes they rented a boat and went fishing out beyond the mouth of the harbor. She was happy, she said, but missed us very much. She hoped we were good boys. In a week she would be home.

An hour after the letter came, we saw John Aldrich coming up the walk. He was Father's attorney, a big, red-faced man with a bristling mustache who used to come to dinner now and then, and who was always cursing Mexico. I didn't like him much, those early years. He was too loud and hearty and he always drank a good deal.

He didn't have to tell us something was wrong that day. We knew. We knew the moment he walked into the patio, and stood frowning at us, not speaking.

"All right," Arthur said. "Tell us." So he told us. There had been a sudden storm in Acapulco Bay. Mother and Father were dead.

I was sixteen then and Arthur was twenty-one. Without him God knows what would have happened to me. He swallowed his grief, pitched in, straightened out Father's tangled affairs and made it possible for us to go on eating and studying. And it was Arthur who, in 1933, got the money together so I could go to Columbia University, and who kept on sending me money until I landed a position teaching English literature, American history and Spanish at the Westchester Academy of Fine Arts.

Sitting there that October morning with his letter in front of me, I knew more clearly than ever that what little I had done I owed to my brother. Had he changed much in these few years, I wondered. When I saw him last he was a giant of a man, beside whom I looked like a bean pole, a big fellow full of laughter with an inordinate fondness for tequila. He said it was the best drink in the world. He said you took a lime and some salt and bottle of tequila, and the first drink you sucked the lime and put salt on your tongue and then drank out of the bottle. After the first drink you threw away the lime and salt.

The nine-o'clock bell rang. I put his letter in my desk, gathered my papers and went down the hall to my classroom, feeling alive for the first time in weeks.

It was in December, around Christmas, that I started worrying about Arthur. I hadn't heard from him, though I had answered his letter, but there was nothing extraordinary about that. Sometimes he wrote once a month—sometimes six or eight months passed before one of his letters turned up. For that matter, his October letter had been his first in almost a year.

Anyway, I had a problem on my hands, a very lovely problem. Her name was Penny Gage.

The term before, she had haunted my office. She used to come in after class and sit in the battered leather chair in the corner and talk to me in halting Spanish. Often she would be waiting to drive me home at four o'clock. I tried to think of her as the child she was, full of hero worship. But I must admit that now and then I played with the thought of having her near me for the rest of my life.

Then suddenly she lost all interest in her studies, and nothing I could do would rekindle that interest. If it had been anyone else but Penny, I would have given the matter no thought at all. But she had shown real promise and the extraordinary change in her attitude toward her work and toward me hurt me a good deal. She never came to my office. She was never waiting to take me home.

I was trying to figure out a new approach to that problem when a brief note from John Aldrich gave me the first hint that all wasn't well with Arthur. Aldrich said he was holding a letter with my return address on it for my brother and wanted to know what to do with it.

I wrote to him at once to try and find Arthur for me. A few days later I thought of an old friend of ours, a newspaperman named Joe Briggs, who had been in Acapulco the day Mother and Father were drowned and who had wired the news to Aldrich. So I wrote to him, too. Then, on the 17th of January, things began to happen.

That day I received the following note from Joe Briggs:

Dear Mitch:

Have they fattened you up any in Westchester and have you learned to comb your hair?

I was in Acapulco doing a bit of fishing and contemplating, as always, the beautiful simplicity of the Mexican electoral system, when your letter arrived. Thus the delay.

I saw Arthur for a few moments when he got back here last October. Now he is not to be found. He hasn't been seen since November 8, and I'm worried as hell. Not by his absence, but because someone else is looking for him and I don't mean John Aldrich.

The guy on Arthur's tail is a dapper, undersized detective who calls himself José Manuel Madero. That is not his name —he's an Indian, a Zapotec, from the hills back of Oaxaca, so you can guess what he was christened. An odd little guy, who, when he gets up against a particularly difficult case, goes home, puts on some of those white pajamas the peons wear, and a pair of huaraches and sits on his haunches in the sun knitting. So far he has knitted a whole sock trying to figure out where in God's name Arthur went. What he wants with your brother he won't say.

I don't like it, Mitchell. There is something very wrong about the whole business. Madero only handles important cases —cases in which the boys upstairs at the Palace are interested. I ran into him first a couple of years ago on a murder case. You may remember—the one where the American girl was murdered in the Palace. An important and entirely innocent Cardenas man would have been hanged for it if Madero hadn't stepped in. Since then he's had the run of the country.

All I know for certain is this. Arthur leased a house on Av. Santa Maria—the one they call the Street of the Crying Woman—late in October, stayed a week or so and disappeared.

Do you know anything that would make this make sense?

Meanwhile I'll keep looking and I'll do my best to break down Señor José's inexplicable reticence.

As ever,

Joe.

Two days after Briggs' letter arrived I had a visitor. He was waiting in the hall outside my study when I came back from lunch, a tall, dark man with a nose that angled off to the left a little. His eyes were big and very sad.

"Dr. Drake?" he asked, as I took out my key and put it in the lock. I nodded.

"My name is Magnin," the man said. There was something odd about his face—a twist to the lower jaw that pulled the corner of his mouth down a bit. The jaw and the nose made the thin face even more striking. At first glance, he seemed to be middle-aged, for his black hair was peppered with gray. A closer inspection told me he was around thirty.

I waved him inside to the chair in the corner, went behind my desk. "What can I do for you?" I asked.

He smiled. The smile took some of the asceticism from his face. Seeing the smile, a woman would have called him sweet. "I understand you're something of an authority on Mexico."

"I used to live there. I've written a couple of books. I'm not—"

He cut the sentence in two. "I've read your Zapata biography. That was a fine job." His tone, more than his words, expressed his admiration.

"Thanks," I said. I liked praise.

"I've done some writing," Magnin said.

Then I knew who he was. Jacques Magnin. *"Bloody Harvest,"* I said and stared across the room at him. It couldn't be. This slim, gentle man with the low, soft voice couldn't be Magnin—Magnin the revolutionary, the organizer, the saboteur. How could that frail body have withstood months of torture at the hands of the Nazis? But there was a fire in him, burning behind his eyes, and there was power in him. I could see it now. And the crooked nose and jaw—he hadn't been born with them. They were mementoes of his work in Germany and France and America.

"You've read it?" He looked pleased.

I said I had. "I should have realized who you were."

"Why?" He smiled again and it wasn't a pleasant smile. "How could you know? Do you realize there's never been a picture of me in the papers?"

I admitted I hadn't seen a picture. I didn't ask why. I didn't need to ask why. He told me anyway.

"I don't allow pictures," Magnin said. "Not from modesty, though. Fear, Dr. Drake. I'm scared to death." He spoke lightly, good-humoredly. He didn't seem afraid, certainly. "You understand?"

I nodded. After all, I had read the book and he gave a good many people plenty of reasons for killing him in that book. I thought of Trotsky. I thought of what had finally happened to Trotsky.

"I was told I could trust you," Magnin said.

"Who?"

"Miss Gage."

I thought he referred to Penny's aunt and guardian, Miss Molly Gage. He didn't, I found out a few days later. He meant Penny. "I'm glad she thinks so."

"I'm going to Mexico City," Magnin went on. "I wondered if you could help me."

"How?"

"You know how it is to go to a strange city."

It occurred to me that Magnin had been to a great many strange cities in his life. However, I got his point. In those days he had people to look up. He didn't now.

"Miss Gage says you have relatives in Mexico."

"I have a brother," I said, forgetting for a minute that I had been in a turmoil for two days because of him.

"Could you give me a letter to him?" It was difficult to say no to that smile. I sensed a sort of helplessness in him.

9

"Do you know anyone else well enough to give me a letter?" He spoke diffidently, as though embarrassed. "An introduction. I don't speak Spanish. I want to rent a little place out of the city somewhere. A quiet place where I can work." He smiled. "Undisturbed," he added. He said the word good-naturedly, yet it had an ominous ring.

"I know a couple of men fairly well," I replied, thinking of John Aldrich and Joe Briggs. "I can send you to them. But you won't need anyone, really. One doesn't need Spanish in Mexico these days. English gets you by nine times out of ten."

"I'd appreciate it, though."

"All right," I said. I picked up a pen and scribbled two short notes. And I did it, not only for Penny's aunt, who was a member of the board of regents of the Westchester Academy of Fine Arts, and who had been very good to me, but for the gentle sad-eyed fellow sitting in front of my desk. I didn't try to analyze my feeling for him. Perhaps I pitied him. For what he had gone through and what he had lost. Faith. I knew he had lost that from his book. And I think that the loss of something to hold on to, something to believe in, is worthy of pity.

Magnin thanked me, tried to crush my hands, smiled again and departed. I thought—a little regretfully—that would be the last I'd see of him. I was wrong.

One night toward the end of January—I think it was the 28th—I went to a faculty dinner. It was late, almost midnight, when I went up the steps of the house in the village where I boarded, let myself in and went softly to my room. My landlady, Mrs. Huntting, was rather strict about her guests, as she called them, frowned on anyone who disturbed the peace and quiet of the place. So I slipped into bed quietly, curbing my temper when my feet pushed out at the end of the bed as they always did—the bed was a bit short for a man who stands six feet two—and went to sleep without even turning on the light.

10

At breakfast Mrs. Huntting looked down her nose at me.

"You went out rather late, didn't you, Professor?"

"It was a bit late," I said. "Faculty meeting." Then I frowned at her. "Went out?"

"Yes. I heard you come in around nine-thirty. Half an hour later you went out again."

"I did nothing of the kind," I said sharply.

The look she gave me said I was lying. I hurried through breakfast and didn't even try to hide my annoyance. I was on the way out when it occurred to me there was something odd about the whole thing. I found out there was. Someone had gone very thoroughly and very carefully through everything I owned. Nothing was missing. Only Arthur's last letter, which I know I had returned to its envelope, wasn't in that envelope now. It was placed neatly on top of the pile of letters in the left-hand bureau drawer and its envelope was under it.

Each day I looked for a letter from John Aldrich and each day I was disappointed. I wrote to him again and tried not to worry. I wrote to Joe Briggs again. Then it was the second week in February and I didn't have much time to worry because there were the mid-term tests to think about.

We used the honor system at Westchester, which was just as well, for it helped many a débutane to graduate from the Academy with high honors. At two o'clock one afternoon I put the members of the class in Spanish in the care of their consciences and went outdoors.

It was a fine bright day, bracingly cold, and I walked briskly across the snow-shrouded campus feeling inside me that sense of freedom that always comes at the end of the term. There was a week ahead of comparative leisure. Winter would soon be over. There would be new faces staring up at me in the classrooms, new voices asking questions—perhaps in the new crop there would be one or two students of promise. One always looked forward to that. I looked up at the gaunt trees and knew they would soon leaf out again and that the grass would be green again.

There was a familiar red Packard convertible nosed against the curb in the space where the girls parked their cars. And seeing it made me warm inside, for it was Penny Gage's car. I stood there looking at it and remembering the day she had driven me to Boston. A fine day. One of those bright days in a man's life. Then I realized I wasn't alone. A man in a blue camel's-hair overcoat and a blue hat with a snap brim was leaning against a tree trunk a few feet away, watching me—a man with the face of an angel.

"Colorful, isn't it?" the man said.

I nodded and felt embarrassed. I wondered if he knew Penny and guessed what my interest in the car was.

"Wouldn't mind owning it," the man said.

"Nor I," I replied, gave him another nod and crossed to the road that led to Woodland. There was a taproom in the village—an eminently respectable one, and that was my destination.

Emil Waller, the pink-cheeked barman, was alone in the pine-paneled room. "Hello, Doc," Emil said. "Playing hookey?"

"Examinations," I explained.

"Don't you watch them wenches?" Emil asked.

"I put them on their honor."

"They didn't do that where I went to school. If they had I would be a bachelor of something or other."

"My students wouldn't think of cheating."

"I'll bet. Do you take their books away from them?"

"And let them feel I don't trust them?"

"Do you?" Emil asked.

"No," I said. "How about a beer?"

"It's too cold for beer," Emil said. "This is whisky-punch weather. I make a very fine whisky punch. I also make a fine whisky sour with rum floated on top of it."

"I have a reputation for sobriety to uphold."

"That's a shame. The whisky sour is wonderful."

"Make me one then."

He grinned and went to work. I put my elbows on the bar and relaxed. There was a mirror in front of me and I looked at myself in it and realized that perhaps the dean was right, perhaps I should get my hair cut oftener. It was straw-colored and gave me a scarecrowish look. Then the mirror said we had company. The young man with the angel face came through the door and put his lean body on a stool to my right. He took off his hat and ran his fingers through his black curly hair.

Emil turned and nodded. "Hello, Angel."

"The name is Paul," the man said.

"That guy last night called you Angel," Emil said.

"To hell with him," the man said. "Give me a Canadian Club straight." There was an ash tray and a box of safety matches on the bar. He took six matches out of the box, began juggling them.

"No you don't," Emil said as he put my whisky sour in front of me. I tasted it. "Good?" Emil wanted to know.

"Wonderful," I said.

"Just one game for a drink." The man who called himself Paul held out three matches.

"I'm a sucker, Doc," Emil said. "I always was." He took the matches. "Watch this, Doc."

"If you're a doctor what's good for a hangover?" Paul asked. He put his hands behind him. Emil did the same thing.

"He isn't that kind of a doctor," Emil said. "He teaches the dames at the Academy. I wish I had me a degree so I could take his job." He whistled, put a closed fist on the bar. "You challenged."

Paul put his closed fist beside Emil's. "Three," Paul said.

"Four." Emil open his fist. There were two matches on his palm.

"A horse on you," Paul said, and showed Emil one match.

"That's an odd game," I said, and moved a little nearer.

13

"They call it the match game," Paul said.

"I think he makes his living at it." Emil put his hands behind him again. So did Paul. This time Emil guesed three.

"None," Paul said and he was right. There were no matches in either palm.

"What did I tell you?" Emil asked. "I should know better after last night. Last night he took me for seven drinks and four bucks."

"One more?" Paul asked.

"Not me," Emil said. "Maybe the Doc will play with you."

"Thanks," I declined.

"How about a drink then?" Paul said.

"No, thanks."

"Some other time, then," Paul said.

"Some other time," I agreed, paid for the sour and headed back for the Academy. And as I walked through the pale sunshine a thought kept pushing itself at me that the man called Paul had followed me to the tavern. But why?

When I reached my office I found a note saying Molly Gage had called and wanted me to call back. I picked up the phone and gave the operator her number.

"Will you come to dinner tonight?" Miss Gage asked.

I said that would be fine. Over the wire her voice was warm.

"Shall I send the car?"

"I can walk."

"And get even thinner?" I heard her low laugh. "No."

"All right, then."

"Seven," Molly Gage said and hung up.

I sat there looking at the phone and thinking of Penny's aunt, and how good she had been to me. One of the nice people in the world—one of the men—or women, rather—of good will. And I was still thinking about her when someone knocked on my door.

"Come in," I said. The door swung open. I took off my glasses and stood up because Penny Gage came in.

14

Until that moment I never realized why it was Penny always made me think of the line from *A Midsummer Night's Dream* which goes "I know a bank where the wild thyme grows." I knew now. She belonged in an enchanted forest. There was something wild and free about her—a slim, golden-haired girl with flecks of gold in her eyes. She had the grace of the barefooted Indian girls you see walking along the mountain trails near Tepozitlan. It was that grace, I think, that made Bernal Diaz speak of them so rapturously four centuries ago. Certainly that's the only beautiful thing about them. Penny carried herself in that same proud way. Only her face wasn't flat and her skin wasn't brown.

"Good afternoon," Penny said. "May I sit down?" She seemed nervous.

"Do, Penny," I said.

She sat in the chair in the corner and tucked her feet under her. We looked at each other. I realized I was wiping my glasses with my fingers so I put them on again and fumbled with the paper knife.

"How did the examination go?"

"I don't know," Penny said.

"Was it too difficult?"

"Pretty difficult."

"I tried not to make it too hard."

"It's my fault," Penny said and found her hands interesting. "I haven't been working."

"Next term you can work harder."

Then she looked up at me. "I've something to ask you."

I jabbed the paper cutter into the blotter. "Yes?"

"Aunt Molly is asking you to dinner tonight."

"She called a short while ago."

"It's about me," Penny said.

"You?"

"She's worried about my state of mind," Penny said.

"I'll assure her—" I wondered what I could assure her about.

"No," Penny said. "You don't need to. I want to go away.

I want to go somewhere and she's going to talk to you about it."

"Why?"

"I'd like to go to Mexico City," Penny said. "I want her to take me there. I don't want to come back here next term."

It didn't make sense. I sat there jabbing the paper cutter into the blotter.

"She thinks Mexico might be dangerous," Penny went on. "She also thinks I should go on to college. But I don't want to now. Would you tell her I ought to go away, that Mexico would be a good place for me, that I could practice my Spanish and see all the places I've been studying about? Would you do that?"

"I suppose it would do you no harm," I said.

She smiled. It was like a light going on. "Oh, thank you."

"Perhaps I should give it a little thought."

"No, please. Please tell her it would be a good idea."

I shrugged. Why not? "All right."

She slid out of the chair and came across to the desk, reached over and patted my hand. "Thank you so very much. I'm to pick you up tonight. I'll be at your house at seven."

I stood up. I wanted to take her hand and squeeze it but it didn't seem the right thing to do. I felt young and a little foolish.

"One more thing." She stood there looking at me. Her eyes made me forget she was—to me at least—a child. Her lips parted a litle and she put up her hand and pushed a strand of hair back.

"Yes," I said.

"If she says anything about Mr. Magnin don't tell her you met him."

Then I began to understand. But it was a little late. By the time I had collected my wits, Penny Gage was gone.

TWO

THERE WAS a piece of moon low in the east that night and a wind blowing. The stars had been thoroughly polished and were bright and cold. Penny was a few minutes late so I sat on the rickety bench on the porch watching the night come down, seeing the lights in the houses along the quiet street turn the windows yellow. I should have been thinking about Arthur. I should have been trying to figure out why Magnin came to see me. All I could think of was Penny and how I would miss seeing her every day.

Presently, a car came along the street, pulled up in front. It was Penny's Packard. She opened the door for me, watched me trying to fit my long legs under the dash.

"Shall I push the seat back?"

"I'm all right."

"It's a wonderful night," she said a little breathlessly. You could tell she was excited and happy.

"Maybe you should finish school, Penny," I said, not looking at her.

She immediately took her foot off the starter. "You wouldn't—"

"No," I said. "I wouldn't. Forget it."

She squeezed my arm, put the car in gear and swung out into the street. Lights flashed behind us but they didn't pass. In the rear-view mirror I could see that there was a car back of us a couple of hundred feet. It kept that distance.

To get to the Gage estate, one went straight out the street on which my boarding house fronted, but Penny didn't go that way. Suddenly she swung right, drove very fast for two blocks, swung left again, circled a block, took a side street for half a mile and shot back into the main road. I gave her a questioning look.

"A game," Penny said.

I took a look in the rear-view mirror. The car wasn't behind us any more.

17

Penny and her aunt lived in a great, rambling brick house on a hill north of town. You left the highway, drove under the railroad and went along a narrow way through the woods and across a little brook. Then you climbed to an iron gate that was always open, through it and along a graveled driveway to the house.

The housekeeper, a plump, gray-haired woman who always smelled of cinnamon, opened the door for us.

"Where have you been?" she wanted to know. "We haven't seen you in a coon's age."

"Martha!" Penny tried to be stern. "Sometimes you're entirely too familiar."

"Why shouldn't I be?" Martha said and nodded toward the living room.

Molly Gage was sitting in front of the fire, reading. She heard us, put the book down and stood up.

As a girl, Penny's aunt must have been startlingly beautiful. She was still lovely, a tall, Junoesque woman with very little gray in her hair, though she must have been fifty. The only wrinkles she had were around her eyes and laughter had put them there. Every time I saw her, I wondered why she hadn't married. The only reason I could think of was that she enjoyed her freedom. She had the merriest eyes I had ever seen—brown eyes with gold flecks in them.

"Hello, Mitch." She came to me and took my hand. "You look gaunt. The brats getting you down?"

"We're not brats," Penny said.

"How he stands it, I don't know," Molly Gage said. "One of you is bad enough. Why don't you get out of it, Mitch? Do something respectable like digging ditches."

"I've thought of it," I said.

"You need a drink," Molly Gage said. "How about a double martini?" There were a pitcher and some glasses on the low table by the chair. She filled three of the glasses, took olives from the dish by the pitcher and dropped them in the glasses.

"They're stuffed, Mitch. Hope you don't mind I can't stand an olive that isn't stuffed."

I took the glass and sat at one end of the davenport and Penny sat at the other. As always, I felt completely at home. I hadn't been in this room for months, but that didn't matter. Molly Gage had that rare quality of making you feel that you belonged.

"We've missed you," Molly Gage said. "Haven't we missed him, Penny?"

"I see him every day," Penny said.

"I've missed you, too," I said.

"Doing any writing?" Penny's aunt asked.

I shook my head. "No time."

"No heart, you mean?"

"Perhaps that's it."

"You mustn't stop work," Penny's aunt said. "You mustn't let that place get you down. Your Zapata book was the best thing I've laid my eyes on in a long while."

"He's blushing," Penny said. "You mustn't praise him because it always makes him blush."

I changed the subject. "How are the dogs?" I asked.

"Millie's having pups," Penny's aunt said. "By the looks of things she'll have ten. She always does."

"Some day I want one," I said.

"Not one of these," Penny's aunt said. "Their father is a scoundrel. Half Scottie, half spaniel, with no sense of responsibility. You hungry?"

"Very," I said.

"Suppose we eat then," said Penny's aunt.

After dinner, we sat near the fireplace, Penny's aunt and I, with the chess board between us. She played well, though she had an odd attitude toward the game—an attitude that reflected her personality, I suppose. It hurt her, she said, that all the pieces, including the queen, should spend their lives defending the lazy king. It would be more fitting if the queen and the king changed places. I asked her once if that meant she thought women should be sheltered. "God forbid," was her reply.

The game was Molly Gage's idea. Penny, at her suggestion, had taken an armful of books back to the rental library in Woodland. She hadn't gone willingly. As she went out, she glanced back at me and I knew she was putting herself completely in my hands.

Miss Gage moved her bishop. "Guard the wench."

I put my knight in front of my queen.

She seemed to be studying the board. But her next remark revealed that her mind wasn't altogether on the game. "I'm sorry she changed," she said. I didn't say anything.

"A hero worshiper," Miss Gage went on. "First it was you. I had you for breakfast and dinner for a year." She moved a pawn, left her queen unguarded.

"I'll take it," I said.

"So you will." She put the pawn back.

"She's very young." It was the only thing I could think of to say.

"So are you."

"I don't feel young."

"Now it's Jacques Magnin," Miss Gage said. "Do you know who he is?"

"Yes." I kept my gaze on the ivory men.

"I don't approve." She castled, then pushed her hair back and smiled at me. "It's none of my business, really. I've led my life. I shouldn't meddle with Penny's. She met him in Maine last summer. He was living in a shack over the hill. He let her read the manuscript of *Bloody Harvest*. That's how it started. Then the book was published and he moved to New York and called her up and she hasn't thought of anything else since."

I started to say that I didn't blame Penny, that I considered Magnin a charming man, but I remembered in time. I said, "I knew something had happened."

"She hasn't been the same, has she?"

I shook my head.

"She's treated you badly, hasn't she?"

"Of course not."

She frowned. "She has. I know she has. She hasn't asked you here in weeks—months."

"Why should—"

She cut the question off. "Why shouldn't she? I don't like it. I don't like Magnin."

"You might go to the Department of Justice and see about having him deported," I suggested. "I doubt if he's a citizen and his passport may be forged."

"Mitch," she said reprovingly. "That's not at all like you." She chuckled. "Anyway, I thought of that first. There's no need now. Two weeks ago he stopped seeing her."

"Then there's nothing to worry about."

"There's Penny. She's desperate, or says she is. I could tell her one gets over such things, but that wouldn't help. It never does. And I don't blame her. Magnin is fascinating. He has courage and—I guess you might say he had integrity. He's a droll fellow. Plenty of humor in him. But his past—I don't like that."

"He tossed that overboard."

"But it hasn't tossed him," said Miss Gage. "Don't you defend him. I don't want him for an in-law." She cocked her head and eyed me with good-natured gravity. "Now you. I never objected to you."

"Anyway, I have no past."

"Perhaps you should have."

"Is she in love with him?" I tried to be casual.

"She thinks she is." Her hand hovered over the board, dropped down and rested on a castle. "She thought she was in love with you once. I'm sorry she changed her mind. Don't blush, Mitch."

I tried to hide my embarrassment. "She got over that. She'll get over Magnin."

"Yes. That's why I'm taking her away. I'm taking her to Mexico. Don't you think it's the right thing to do?"

"Yes," I agreed.

"Would you like to go with us, Mitch?"

"Me?"

"You," Miss Gage said. "I can get a leave of absence for you. And you're in check."

I interposed my black knight. "I don't think I can go."

"It would do you good." Her gaze swept my face. "Somehow you appeal to me as an unhappy young man. I don't blame you. You aren't a teacher, not really."

"I know it," I said. "But one must eat."

"There'll be plenty of room in the car for you."

"Thanks. I'll think it over. It's nice of you to want me."

"I need someone to play chess with. Think it over hard. And you're going to lose your queen, so think about that too."

It was after ten when I went home. Penny had returned just before nine and had sat watching us, not saying anything because she played chess too and knew better than to comment on moves. She drove me home and not until we reached my gate did she speak. She took my hand and held it.

"You're a dear."

"Thanks."

"You think I'm being bad."

"No."

"But you do."

"No," I said. "No, Penny."

"Try and understand."

"All right."

"I'll miss you," Penny said.

"I'll miss you too," I said.

"Good-by, Dr.— Mitchell." She pressed my hand hard. I got out of the car. She smiled and waved and I stood at the gate and watched her drive away. Then I turned and went up the icy walk feeling lonely and lost and let myself quietly into the house. Under my door was an envelope. It had John Aldrich's return address on it.

I tore it open, stood in the middle of the dingy room reading it. Then I stopped thinking about Penny. For Aldrich said I must come to Mexico City at once. He said he was certain something had happened to Arthur. He said if I needed money to wire him and he would send it.

Two days later I was on a plane and the plane was bound for the airport which stands on the dry bed of the lake the Aztecs called Texcoco.

THREE

THERE WAS a traffic jam at the corner of Uruguay and Avenida Cinco de Febrero. Men sat at the wheels of their cars, put their hands on the horns and let them stay there. It didn't untangle the jam but it made a lot of noise, and that seemed to satisfy the horn blowers.

It was a fine clear day with not much wind, and where the sun spilled on the pavement it was warm. I came out of the Hotel Ontario and stood in the sun feeling strange and a little lost. The city had changed. I knew it when I awakened that first morning. For one thing, there were no bells. In the old days that's the thing you noticed most in the morning, bells ringing everywhere. And there were too many cars and there were too many neon signs and there were too many traffic signals and too many radio stores with the radios standing out in front turned on full blast.

I moved down to the corner and then I saw what was causing the tieup. A car was parked on the street-car tracks which at this point were laid close to the curb and an electric engine with a flat car behind it couldn't make the turn.

No one was angry. No one was particularly excited. The drivers sat placidly in their cars and smoked and blew their horns. Two policemen leaned against the corner of a hardware store studying the situation through a cloud of smoke. The motorman sat on the steps of his equipage, yawning now and then, Around the parked car there was a crowd of men and boys, and some old women and little girls were going through the crowd selling lottery tickets.

After a while the motorman walked over to the crowd and held a conference about what was the best thing to do. It seemed that the owner of the car was nowhere to be found. Then the policemen went over and joined the group. I followed and for the first time I began to feel at home. It was the smell of Mexican cigarettes, the smell of smoke and dust and the sound of all those soft voices.

"Perhaps we should move the car," the motorman suggested.

"But the owner," one of the men protested. "He may object."

"He should not have left it there," one of the policemen pointed out.

"How was he to know this train would come?"

"There are tracks," the policeman said.

"But they are seldom used."

The policemen considered the matter, scowled at the motorman. He shrugged. "I could not help it," he said. "They sent me with the train."

"Move the car and put it back," suggested a by-stander.

Everyone smiled and nodded. Twenty or thirty men picked the automobile up, lifted it onto the pavement. The motorman got back into his train and went on past. Then the men returned the car to its original position with a great deal of good-natured laughter.

I stood there smiling at them. Only in Mexico could something like that happen. The city might change but its people wouldn't. Nothing would change them—nothing ever had. A small dirty hand pulled at my trousers. A thin voice told of the wealth that would be mine if I purchased one tiny ticket.

I gave the girl fifty centavos and put the ticket in my pocket, moved west on Uruguay. Two men came toward me carrying a bed on their heads. A turkey sat on a window sill eating corn. One leg was tethered to a nail in the sill. I went on to the corner where an old woman was cooking tacos over a charcoal brazier, and turned east. When I came to Avenida Madero I went west again and presently I was at Number 86. Joe Briggs was waiting for me in the entrance of the old building.

"Just as thin as ever," Joe said. "Thinner, if that's possible."

"Hello, Joe," I said. He hadn't changed much. There was no gray in his sandy hair and he was as lithe as a boy of twenty. He was past fifty, I knew that, for the first time I saw him in 1925 I thought of him as old. I don't remember asking him how long he had been in Mexico. But I know he interviewed Villa once when Pershing was chasing him, and he was in the city when Villa and Zapata rode into town side by side, and he was at Vera Cruz when the marines landed.

"Good to see you, Mitch. Sorry I was out last night."

"I should have wired. Any news?"

He shrugged. "Nope."

I told him about Aldrich's letter. "That's why I hurried down."

"You seen him yet?"

"No. Talked to him on the phone last night."

"What's he in such an uproar about?" Joe asked. "I saw him only last week and he wasn't excited then."

"He didn't say. Suppose we find out." I led the way down the hall to the ancient elevator. There was a door at the right of the shaft. It was open. A woman sat at a desk sewing. She smiled at us.

"Three," I told the operator.

Joe squeezed my arm. "A hell of a long time," Joe said. "Six—seven years."

"Eight. How was Arthur when you saw him?"

"Swell. Getting fat."

"Do you think anything's happened to him, Joe?"

"I don't see what. Let's not worry, kid."

We got out of the elevator, went down the hall and pushed open a door with John Aldrich's name on it. It was the same office the attorney had occupied when I was a boy, a high-ceilinged room with immense windows and the same withered little man named Ramon de Silva at a desk by the windows.

Ramon got up, came around the desk and peered at me through his thick-lensed glasses.

"It is," he said, and held out his hand. "The thin one. The one who calls himself Mitchell. Yes?"

"Yes," I said.

"So long," Ramon said. "So very long." He shook my hand hard, then led us to the door into the inner office, opened it and stood aside.

John Aldrich stood back of his desk, beaming, a big ruddy man with a thin mustache that was peppered with gray. He had always reminded me of the English majors in the Kipling stories— a roast-beef, Yorkshire-pudding sort of fellow. Yet he wasn't English and he didn't like to be called English. As usual, he looked well fed, prosperous and heading for early apoplexy. "Mitch," he boomed. "By God, Mitchell. Look just like your father. A string bean. A scarecrow. But then you always did. Older. Been around a bit. Remember playing all over this office?"

"I remember. You look well."

"Always am well. Always have been well. It's the food. Mostly bad. Then you don't eat so much. Right, Joe?"

"Right," Joe said. He sat down and lit a cigarette. I straddled a chair and leaned on the back of it and tried not to seem upset when Aldrich rambled on about Father and Mother and about the old days, the good old days of Don Porfirio Diaz.

It was Joe who stopped him. Joe didn't like Diaz' memory any better than I did. The only Mexican president Joe liked to remember was Juarez and he used to say that if he had lived in Juarez's time he probably wouldn't have liked him much either. "What's happened about Arthur?" Joe wedged the question in when Aldrich paused to light his pipe.

"Of course," Aldrich said. "Sorry, Mitch. You must be worried. It's a woman."

"Woman?" Joe repeated.

Aldrich nodded. "A dancer at the El Toro. She is Arthur's girl."

"Which one?" Joe asked.

"The American," Aldrich said. "The blonde—Dorothy Allen."

"I've seen her," Joe said.

"What about her?" I got up and leaned on Aldrich's desk.

"She and Arthur were going to be married," Aldrich said gravely. "They were going to be married February 5. I just found it out. And the way she is carrying on, I'm damned sure something is seriously wrong."

"Has she seen him?"

"Not since November."

"How did you find out about this?" Joe asked. He was sitting on the edge of the leather couch, scowling at Aldrich.

"She came to me."

"When?"

"The day I wrote Mitch. Friday, I guess it was."

"Why so long?" Joe said. "Why didn't she come before?"

Aldrich's eyes were thoughtful, worried. "She said when Arthur didn't show up to marry her she didn't know who to go to. Then she suddenly remembered Arthur speaking about me so she came up. Said she got a letter from him in December so that's why she didn't worry before."

"A letter?" I said.

"From Vera Cruz." Aldrich opened a drawer, took out a piece of blue notepaper, put it in my hand. It was from Arthur. There was no doubt of that. I knew his scrawl too well to doubt its authenticity. It ran:

Dec. 28.

Dot Darling:

I wanted to be with you at Christmas, but there was nothing I could do about it, so I had to try to make up for it by sending the very unworthy gift. Next year it will be something bigger and finer — you understand, I know.

If it helps any, I'm not having fun. I never liked Vera Cruz — never will like it. But I have to stay a while longer. With luck, I'll be back by the middle of January. But don't be upset if I fail to show until just before our day — the biggest day in our lives. I've put a red ring around the date. And from now on we can join the Mexicans in celebrating El Cinco de Febrero.

I've told no one about us yet — not even Mitch. You see how I keep promises, darling. It has been a great temptation, but you know best.

Do you know how very much I love you? And how very much I miss you? Days pass quickly. Soon you'll be in my arms and then you'll never leave them.

            Your
               Arthur

I gave the letter to Joe. He read it, got up then and stood staring at a big photograph of the pyramid at Cholula. He said, without turning: "Maybe that explains his absence. Maybe he ran out on the dame."

"Not Arthur," I said. "He wouldn't do that. If he had decided to back out, he would have come back and told her so."

"I suppose so," Joe agreed.

"The day after I wrote you I flew to Vera Cruz," Aldrich put in. "I couldn't find a trace of him. He must have stayed with friends or in some little dump of an inn because he hadn't been at any of the hotels."

"Did you go to the police?" I asked.

"They came to me. Not there. Here."

"Madero?" Joe wanted to know.

Aldrich nodded. "He's been here twice."

"Did you show him the letter?" Joe turned, faced us.

"Of course not. Should I?"

"No," Joe said. "Not until we find out what they want with Arthur. Any idea, Johnny?"

"Not the vaguest—unless—"

"Unless what?" I asked.

"Unless he's done something to displease the boys in the Palace. What do you think, Joe?"

"It's something serious or Madero would tell me," Joe replied. "He trusts me—always has. But I can't pry one hint out of him about this. It isn't murder, because no one who means anything has been knocked off recently. I looked into that. And it has nothing to do with the Bureau of Anthropology. Even the new chief at Guadalajara has nothing but praise for him."

I took Arthur's last letter from my pocket and tossed it to Joe. "Maybe the answer is there."

He read it, gave it to Aldrich. "See what you make of it, Johnny."

Presently Aldrich looked up. "What makes you think the answer is here, Mitch?"

I told him about the night my room was searched. "Whoever did it, read the letter."

"It doesn't make sense to me." Aldrich knocked his pipe on the edge of the wastebasket, stuffed more tobacco in the bowl.

"He was on the trail of something," Joe said. "I suppose the thing to do is find out what."

"That's a big order." Aldrich sighed. I thought he looked tired, suddenly.

Joe stood up, tossed his half-finished cigarette out the window. "This is getting us nowhere. I've work to do, anyway. Have to see Comacho. I'll nose around this afternoon. Call you around six, Mitch. We'll have dinner." He grinned and I felt better. It meant a great deal to have someone like Joe at your elbow when you needed him. He was so capable and dependable and he didn't let things stampede him. I knew if there was any way to get to the bottom of Arthur's disappearance, Joe would find it.

"Think I should see Madero?" I asked.

"You'll see him soon enough. He's probably on your tail right now." Joe smiled again and was gone.

"There goes a fine fellow," Aldrich said.

"A swell one," I said. "Where shall I start, John?"

"You might talk to Ruiz. He's at the Regis. It won't do any good because I talked to him and Joe talked to him. But he's Arthur's friend and it might cheer you up. And you can go out to the house Arthur leased. You know where it is?"

"The Street of the Crying Woman," I said.

He nodded. "His things are there and you better go through them. I haven't done that. Didn't feel I should. Sort of intruding."

"Intruding hell," I said. "Thanks, John."

"I haven't done anything."

"Well, you tried. That's a lot." We shook hands.

"You better look up the girl," he added. "You'll find her at the El Toro."

"I'll do that," I said and left him.

I went downstairs feeling fairly cheerful. Everything was going to be all right. I was sure of that. Seeing Joe and John Aldrich gave me a fine hopeful sense. But when I reached the street I didn't feel hopeful any more. A man came along Madero carrying a coffin on his shoulder.

FOUR

THERE WAS about the Hotel Regis an air that was entirely

Mexican. Its glory had faded, with the gilt in the dining rooms where generals had once fired .38 caliber bullets into the pictures on the walls. Not very often now did the feet of the mighty wear down the nap of the carpets in the lobby. An era had gone and with it some of the splendor of that big hotel on Avenida Jaurez.

When I entered the place I looked around for some familiar face, but none was there. I went over to the elevator and waited for a car.

"Mister," a voice asked in English. "You want to get upstairs?"

A youthful bell boy was standing beside me, grinning.

I replied in Spanish. Certainly I wanted to go up. Was there anything preventing me?

He beamed. Certainly not. The upstairs was mine. The only trouble was, he pointed out, the electricity was off.

"At eleven off goes the juice," he said. "At eleven sharp. Not until two does it return."

"Why?"

He shrugged. "They say the drought. They say the water shortage."

"You do not approve?"

"It is I who must run up seven or eight flights twenty times a day. Would you approve?"

"I suppose not."

"You are no tourist?"

"No."

"Good," the bell boy said. "I do not like tourists, though they tip well. Women mostly, who chatter like crows. Teachers."

"I am a teacher."

"But not a woman," the bell boy said. "There are the stairs."

I walked up the seven flights slowly because of the altitude. It would be some days, I knew, before my heart and lungs grew accustomed to it. I found Ruiz's door, knocked and waited.

"Come," a voice called in Spanish.

I opened the door and faced a slim, small man with a white skin and a black, carefully trimmed mustache.

"So wonderful to meet you," Ruiz said after I introduced myself. He extended a soft, carefully manicured hand. His smile was all white teeth and he spoke English with no trace of an accent.

"It's good to see you," I said. "Arthur spoke of you often."

"A fine fellow, Arthur. Sit down, won't you?"

I sat in the one chair and he sat on the bed. The room looked out on Juarez and even with the window closed you could hear the steady clamor of automobile horns. Ruiz seemed not to notice the noise. Whether he was used to it, or whether he had something more important to worry over, I couldn't tell. It occurred to me that he was distraught.

I took Arthur's last letter from my pocket and gave it to him. He read it, his face impassive, then gave it back.

"You know your brother," he said. "Full of plans—schemes." He smiled then. "Like all of us, I suppose. I don't think this"—he meant the letter—"is of any consequence."

"He wrote it just before he disappeared," I pointed out.

"Your brother"—he waved his hand—"don't worry about him. He's not far away."

"I hope not," I said and then I asked him about the dancer, Dorothy Allen. "Did you know they were to be married?" I asked.

"Mr. Aldrich told me. I didn't know until then. I admit I was surprised. I was, at first, a little hurt that Arthur had said nothing about it."

"He said nothing about it to me," I said.

"I suppose he had his reasons."

"I suppose so too," I said. From the letter I took it that his reason was Miss Allen. Apparently she wanted it kept a secret. I got up. "I must go."

"Anything I can do," Ruiz said, and shook my hand hard.

"Anything. You see, I like your brother very much."

"Thanks," I said.

I caught a bus outside the hotel. It was jammed and I had to stand and try to keep my feet as the driver sent the vehicle roaring along the street as though his life depended on breaking all records for the run. A woman in front of me had a little pig in her lap and the pig was asleep. I was the only one on the bus who seemed at all nervous as we swooped around corners and did our best to remove fenders from other buses. Finally I had enough of it and got off. It was good to walk the few remaining blocks to Arthur's house. Anyway, it was a whole lot safer.

Walking along Puente de Alvarado I thought of my childhood. When we were boys, Arthur and I used to play a game whenever we were in the vicinity of Pedro de Alvarado's prodigious—and probably exaggerated—leap as he fled from the Aztecs. Arthur was always one of the Spaniards—sometimes Cortez, sometimes Alvarado—and I was an Indian. He galloped along on an imaginary horse and I ran after him shooting imaginary arrows, but he always got away. We used to sit on the spot where we thought the broad canal must have been and ponder over what happened to the gold the Spaniards dropped in their flight. Arthur was certain it was under us somewhere and that if we dug up the street we could find at least a portion of Montezuma's legendary treasure.

It seemed to me fitting—and a little touching—that Arthur's house should be in the vicinity of the place where we played that game so many times. Santa Maria, too, was a familiar street. I had always loved the legend that made people forget its real name and call it the Street of the Crying Woman—the ghost of Dona Marina—La Malinche—Cortez's mistress, roaming the narrow way, weeping, always weeping. Come back from the other world to do penance because she had betrayed her people, the Aztecs. La Calle de La Llorona. A lovely name.

The house was typical of the Mexican middle class, a wall facing the street, a door opening into a passageway that led to the patio. It was floridly furnished and there were two awful pictures of cherubs in the living room and a plaster saint in a niche in the corner. A man and woman, more Spanish than Indian, let me in and when they found out who I was they started fluttering around me, offering me pan dulce and aguardiente. The woman was called Juanita. Her husband said he was Pablo Guzman, a man of great talent on the trumpet.

"Not at all like your brother," Juanita said. "Not one bit like your brother."

"Why should he be?" Pablo wanted to know.

"They are brothers."

"My brother and I are brothers," said Pablo. "Do we look alike? Can he play the trumpet?"

After half an hour with them I formed the opinion that Arthur's judgment of servants was bad. I didn't like them. I didn't trust them. It seemed to me—even when I was alone in his bedroom—that they were close by, watching and spying. Yet I couldn't blame them for that. After all, they were in charge of the place.

My search of the house told me absolutely nothing. His clothes were there. His books were there. His papers were there but there was no clue to his whereabouts. On the dresser top were three pictures. One was of Father and Mother sitting in a carriage and smiling. It was the last picture taken of them, I remembered. Another was a snapshot of myself, taken at Columbia. The third, in a silver frame, was of a girl in a languorous pose, with her pale hair cascading back and a froth of chiffon across her breast. "For my darling, from Dorothy," she had written across one corner. So that was Dorothy. There was no denying her beauty. If she was anything like her photograph you couldn't blame Arthur for loving her. Fear tugged at my heart. Where was he? What had happened to him? And worry drove me from the room and from the house.

I walked east on Puente de Alvarado feeling helpless and useless. There must be something I could do to find him. Somewhere in this sprawling city there must be someone who could give me a clue. For all the good I was doing, I might as well have stayed at the Academy. At least I was earning money there.

I reached the Zocalo and crossing it remembered that when I was little there were trees growing in the square, but there weren't any now. There were only buses and more buses and street cars and people walking slowly in the sun. The cathedral looked dismally decrepit, as though it had given up its struggles against the shifting sands underneath and the shifting times above. I crossed to the Palace, went past a knot of soldiers and into a court. There were stairs in front of me, so I climbed them and leaned on the rail looking at the Rivera mural. In the state of mind I was in, the mural was a good idea. It took my thoughts away from my own problems and put them on the violent, bloody past of Mexico.

A soft voice intruded. "Perhaps I could explain the mural?"

At my elbow was a dapper little man with eager brown eyes. He had the high cheekbones and the brown skin of the Indian. His straight black hair was plastered neatly back. In his hand was a pearl gray hat. His suit was of green gabardine, his tie was green and out of his breast pocket peeked a green handkerchief. You could see your face in his tan shoes.

"I understand it perfectly," I said irritably.

"I beg your pardon."

"That's perfectly all right."

"Perhaps you mistook me for a guide?"

"Aren't you?"

"A government employee, yes. A guide, no. We must watch the mural closely. Vandals." He pointed to a spot low down on the left where the figure of a priest was blurred. "Acid. A fanatic tried to destroy Mr. Rivera's work."

"So they deprive you of the siesta," I said.

"There is no siesta for us who work for the government now." He smiled. "The new oder." His shrug was expressive. "So you understand this?" He embraced the picture with a gesture.

"Yes."

"Do you approve?"

"It is history."

"Not all of it." The little man nodded toward the top of the left panel. "Mr. Rivera theorized a bit there. Are you, by chance, a student?"

"Something like that," I said.

"You live here?"

"At the moment."

"It is a great country."

"A fine country."

"It will be greater, some day. At the moment we are a little confused, I think. We move forward, then back a bit. You have read much about us?"

"A good deal."

"We have had noble men—Hidalgo, Jaurez." He hesitated. Then added another name—"Zapata—Emiliano Zapata."

The mention of that name let down the bars. I smiled at him and in a moment we were deep in a discussion of Mexican politics and now we used his language. At first I was rusty, for the Spanish I had taught at the Academy was more Castilian than Mexican. Presently he put on his hat and said he must go.

"You trust me with the mural then?"

"Oh yes."

"I hope to see you again," I said.

"Oh, you will." He beamed at me. "You most certainly will. Good day, sir." And with that he went rapidly down the stairs and disappeared. It occurred to me then that I had forgotten to ask his name. But it would be no task to find him if he worked in the Palace. I left the place telling myself that when I had nothing else to do I must come back. Talking to someone like the little man in green was a pleasure not often granted to me.

From the hotel I called Joe, but he was out. Then I called

Aldrich. He had nothing to report. So I lay down on the long, low bed and then I realized how tired I was. The altitude always did that to me the first few days. I closed my eyes.

The telephone bell awakened me. I glanced at my watch, saw it was five. Joe was on the other end of the wire.

"Meet me at my place in an hour or so," Joe said.

"Anything new?"

"I don't know yet. I'm going to see someone. Then I'll know."

"All right," I said, trying to keep excitement down. "In an hour."

I lay back feeling hopeful. I wondered who Joe was going to see and why. Maybe the woman, Dorothy. If not, I would see her tonight. Perhaps we could see her together. I thought about Joe trying to help me and the thought filled me with warmth. He had always been good to me and to Arthur. Particularly after Father and Mother died. That's when I had really started knowing him. He had taken us under his wing, so to speak. Once he said he had adopted us in his mind, that he had taken us and made us his family.

Presently I took a shower and changed my clothes. Outside the hotel a boy with a shine box in his hand barred my way. He pointed to my dusty shoes.

"Shine, boss?"

"Yes," I said. I leaned against the building and put my foot on the box. "You speak English?"

"Sure."

"You learn it at school?"

"Naw," the boy said. "From peectures. The ones that move."

"You like pictures?"

"You bet." He slapped polish on my shoes. "The bang-bang ones. Bogart I like. A tough guy. A very tough guy." He made a sound like a machine gun.

"As tough as Pancho Villa?"

"That one," the boy said disgustedly. "A bandit." I listened to him talk and watched the people moving by. It was clouding over and there was the feel of rain in the air. But it wasn't cold. I was grateful for that. I had had enough cold.

"Ten cents," the boy said.

I gave him a ten-centavo piece and he scowled at me. "That's two cents."

"And you call Villa a bandit," I said in Mexican.

His face lit up. "No tourist, señor. I will not show you the dirty pictures then."

I grinned back at him. "It would be useless." I gave him five centavos more and went along the street.

It was after six when I reached Joe's apartment house, a new one back of the Fronton. He lived one flight up. I climbed the stairs and put my finger on the button, heard the bell ringing inside. But no one answered it. So I tried the door. It was open. I turned the knob and stepped inside.

Then I knew why Joe hadn't answered the bell. He couldn't. He was dead. He was lying face down on the couch near the window that looked out on the street and there was a knife in his back.

A wave of grief and horror engulfed me and Joe's death wasn't the only reason for it. The hilt of that knife was a magnet that drew me closer and closer to the couch where the body lay.

There was no mistaking that knife, for the handle was covered with pesos, crudely hammered out and fitted together. I had made the knife for my brother fifteen years before and it was the sort of a weapon only a boy who had reveled in H. Rider Haggard, whose great hero was Alan Quartermain, would have conceived. The blade was a thin piece of obsidian I had found near the Temple of Quetzalcoatl—a bit of stone which Arthur had said had been a sacrificial knife centuries ago. I had made the hilt of silver dollars and had fitted it on the stone shaft. If you twisted it a certain way, the blade and the hilt parted and in the space inside I had carefully engraved my brother's name. At the time that had seemed highly appealing to me—like a secret passageway or a secret drawer in an old desk.

How long I stood there, I didn't know. All the past came up to swirl around me, to make what confronted me unreal. It can't be, I found my mind saying. It can't be. It can't be.

But it was. I knew it only too well when I heard a footstep behind me. I swung around.

Facing me was the little man in green.

"I told you I would see you again," he said. "You see, I am José Manuel Madero."

FIVE

THERE WAS José Manuel Madero leaning against the door looking at me, his brown face expressionless, and there on the couch was Joe's body, and there was the knife I had made from a handful of pesos and a needle-sharp piece of stone. Night was coming down slowly and softly and now and then a few drops of rain fell.

"I didn't kill him," I said.

"Of course not," José Manuel Madero said. "Of course you didn't kill him."

I had to talk to keep from thinking. I had to find words and put them together into sentences, though I knew what I was saying was stupid.

"The door was unlocked and I walked in," I said. "He asked me to have dinner with him so I came up and rang the bell and then I came in and found him."

The little detective moved away from the door, crossed the room and stood looking down at the body. "Curious. The knife. A curious weapon."

I could have told him I had made the knife. I didn't.

"So crude," Madero said.

"Yes," I said.

I remembered standing at the work bench hammering away at the silver disks, trying to fit them together. I remembered finding the sliver of stone in a pile of rubble in the shadow of the pyramid at Teotihuacan. I remembered Arthur's pleased smile when I gave him the knife.

"Almost the work of a child," Madero said. He touched Joe's cheek with the fingers of his right hand and the gesture was so gentle it was almost a caress. Then he took a gold cigarette case from his pocket and held it out. I took a cigarette and lit it, trying to hold my hand steady.

"Sit down, please," Madero said.

I sat. But the chair faced the couch and I didn't want to look at the couch. I moved the chair around.

"Why was he murdered?" Madero asked.

I shook my head. "I don't know."

"Death needs a reason, Dr. Drake."

"I don't know," I repeated.

"Where is your brother, Dr. Drake?"

"That's why I'm here," I said. "I'm looking for him."

"And he was helping you?" he indicated Joe's body.

"Yes."

Madero wasn't looking at me. He was staring at the window. It was dark outside now and you couldn't see the Monument to the Revolution any more. "Mr. Briggs called me shortly before six and asked me to come here. He said he thought he knew where your brother was."

I pulled smoke into my lungs. Behind me was Joe's body and the knife I had given Arthur was in Joe's back. I didn't say anything.

"You know, of course, I am deeply interested in finding your brother."

"Joe said—" His name choked me. I had to pull the rest of the sentence out. "You were. He said he didn't know why."

"He didn't," Madero said.

"Why do you want Arthur?"

He ignored the question. "Do you think your brother murdered Mr. Briggs?"

"No," I cried. "No. I don't think that."

"The knife—have you seen it before?"

"No."

"I wondered," he said softly. "When I entered this room it seemed as if you were standing there staring at the knife."

"I was staring at Joe," I said. "I was trying to make myself believe it hadn't happened."

"Tell me everything you know, Dr. Drake."

The cigarette was burning my fingers. I got up and went over to the table and put the butt in an ash tray. Standing by the table I couldn't see the couch and I couldn't see Madero. I said, "I haven't heard from my brother since last October. Then John Aldrich wrote me and wanted to know where he was. I wrote to Aldrich and to Joe to try and find Arthur. They couldn't. There was some research I wanted to do here and I was worried about Arthur, so I came down. That's all I know."

"That isn't much."

"No. It isn't much."

"You talked to Mr. Briggs tonight?"

"At five. He called and said to meet him here."

"Is that all he said?"

"He said he was going to see someone."

"He didn't say who?"

"Perhaps he meant you."

"He didn't mean me," Madero said.

"Who then?"

"Your brother perhaps."

I swung around. "Arthur didn't kill him. Arthur and I felt the same way about Joe. No. Arthur wasn't here."

"How do you know?"

"I don't know." My voice was loud, strident. It didn't seem to come from my throat at all. I stared across the room at the little man in green, at the mask of impassivity that was his face and then I remembered what Joe had said about him, how he dressed like a peon and sat against a wall knitting. "What has Arthur done?" I asked. "You can tell me that."

41

"No," Madero said. "Not now."

"But he didn't do this. I tell you he didn't do this."

"You may go," Madero said. "You are upset now. Tomorrow morning we will talk again."

"All right," I said. "I'm at the Ontario hotel."

"Yes," Madero said. "Good night."

"Good night," I said, and went out. Two blocks away there was a store and a sign on the store said there were telephones inside. I went in and called Aldrich's office, but there was no one in. Then I looked through the book and found his name and called his apartment.

"Joe's dead," I told him when he came to the phone. I felt numb and cold. "Joe's been murdered."

"Oh my God," Aldrich said.

"Madero's there now. He thinks Arthur is mixed up in it."

"That's ridiculous."

"Joe was killed with Arthur's knife," I said.

"No, no." Aldrich seemed to be trying to convince himself it wasn't true.

"Yes."

"Does Madero know it was Arthur's knife?"

"No. I didn't tell him. I told him as little as possible."

"How little was that?"

I repeated the story I had given Madero. I could hear the attorney take a deep breath. "Don't say anything more than you have to," he counseled. "If Arthur is in it, we've got to help him."

"I know it."

"You don't think—"

"No, I don't think," I said. "I don't care what Arthur has done."

"Neither do I," Aldrich said. "Do as little talking as possible. Keep out of Madero's way if you can. He'll be in to see me, probably. I'll tell him just what you did. Now you get something to eat and go to bed."

"I'm going to see the girl first," I said.

"All right. But be careful. They'll have men watching you."

"I'll be careful," I said.

I couldn't eat. I went into Henry's and looked at the bill of fare, but the thought of food made me ill. So I had a martini and went outside. There was a man looking at lottery tickets in a window a few doors away and when I started toward Jaurez he followed. I turned east and a couple of blocks away I saw a taxi stalling along beside me so I got in and told the driver to take me to the hotel. It was still raining a little but it was a warm rain.

I told the clerk to call me at seven-thirty, got my key and took the old elevator upstairs. But I didn't stay in my room. I turned on the light, went out again and walked down. In the lobby the man who had followed me was sitting on the couch reading a paper. I went back past the elevator and through a door into a passageway and down the passageway to another door that let me into an alley. Then I walked rapidly south for two blocks, took a westbound bus and got off at San Juan de Letran. Half a block up I stopped and bought some cigarettes and made sure I had lost my shadow. Then I cut over to Aranda and went along it until I found the El Toro. There was a neon sign over the entrance showing a bull chasing a matador.

The orchestra members had on charro costumes and were playing the *Indian Love Call,* giving it a Mexican flavor. It wasn't good. A waiter who looked like Carranza wanted to give me a table in the middle of the small, crowded room but I ignored him, found an empty booth in the corner, and sat down.

"Wheesky?" the waiter asked. "I used to work in Detroit for Meester Ford. How do you like Mexico city, huh? You want a girl?"

"No," I said. "Beer."

"Okeh," the waiter said. "Beer. Okeh." He bounced away.

The place was nearly filled and most of the people were tourists and you could see they were trying desperately to have fun. It reminded me of all the pseudo-Mexican places in New York. I took a piece of paper from my pocket and wrote a note to Dorothy Allen and when the waiter came with the beer I put it in his hand and put a fifty-centavo piece on top of it.

"Give this to Miss Allen," I told him in Mexican. He went away. A little later I saw him beckoning from the door that led into the back so I got up and crossed the room and went through the door and down a hall that smelled of cheap perfume and onions.

"In there." The waiter pointed to another door. "She says to go in."

It was a tiny room with a couch, a chair and a dressing table in it. She was standing by the dressing table, tall and slim and very lovely. She wasn't wearing very much. Both her hands went out to me and I took them and tried not to look at her too hard because I didn't want to embarrass her. Then I remembered that dancers were supposed to show their bodies so I tried to be matter of fact about it.

"So you're Mitchell." Her voice was low and pleasantly husky. I saw that her eyes were topaz and very large.

"Yes," I said.

"You don't look like Art at all. Yes you do. The mouth is the same when you smile." She sat down and put a little frown between her eyes. "I'm scared stiff, Mitchell."

"So am I," I said.

"I love him very much," Dorothy Allen said. "What's happened to him, Mitchell?"

"I don't know."

"We've got to find him. I can't stand it much longer. I'm glad you're here. It makes me feel better that you're here. I didn't know what the hell to do, really I didn't."

"I suppose not," I said and tried to smile.

"But it's better now you're here." She smiled back. I saw how long her lashes were.

"No, it's not," I said. "It's much worse."

The smile went away. "Something's happened to him?"

"Not to him. To Joe Briggs?"

"Who?"

"A friend of Arthur's and mine. A newspaperman."

She put her hand over her mouth.

"He was murdered tonight," I said.

Her hand stifled a cry.

"And I'm afraid the police think Arthur had something to do with it."

"He couldn't. Oh, he couldn't."

"I know he couldn't. But that's what they think just the same."

"Oh my God," Dorothy Allen said. She put her blond head on her arms and began to cry.

"Don't, please." I got up and stood by her awkwardly, not knowing what to do. "Please, Miss Allen. Don't."

"All right." She sat up and took a deep breath. "Sorry. Tell me about it."

I told her. Only I didn't tell her about the knife. I knew Madero would find her eventually and I didn't want her to know that the knife was the one I had made for my brother. I knew he would pry it out of her.

"You think the murder has something to do with Arthur?"

I nodded. "It seems so."

"Would it help if I talked to them?"

"You wait," I said. "They don't know about you yet. Only Aldrich and Ruiz know about you."

She pushed her hair back. It made me think of the piles of corn you see at the edge of the mitlas in the autumn. "It's my fault. I should have married him last summer. I was a fool. An awful fool."

"No," I said.

"But I was. I said to wait. He wanted to get married then. He didn't have much money and I had this job and I have to send money home, so I wouldn't. They don't want married women here. And I wouldn't let him tell anyone about us."

"He didn't even tell me."

"I know he didn't. He promised not to tell anyone. He always keeps his promises. What are we going to do, Mitchell?"

I wished I knew the answer to that question. I didn't. I was floundering around without the slightest idea what to do or where to go. I didn't know even why I was in Dorothy Allen's dressing room. Only seeing the girl Arthur loved made me feel a little closer to him. "Why did he go to Vera Cruz?"

"He said on business."

"Did he say what business?"

She shook her head.

"After he quit the bureau did you know what he planned to do?"

Again she shook her head. "He was—well—mysterious."

"Did he say anything about making a lot of money?"

"Yes."

"But he didn't say how he was going to make it?"

"No."

"I've got to have something to work on," I said. "Some place to begin. I've got to find out where he is and who killed Joe. And I don't know how to go about it."

She made a gesture of helplessness, turned and sat looking in the mirror for a moment, then mechanically began putting on makeup. Her back was fine and straight and very white and her shoulders sloped a little. There was a tiny mole on her right shoulder blade. I liked the way her hair lay on her neck. She frowned at her image.

"There was something about a book," she said. "An old book."

I waited, watching her. It seemed right that I was in the room, as though she were part of my family, as though I were sitting in the same room with Arthur's wife.

"It was in Guadalajara," Dorothy Allen said. "That's where I met him. In the spring I met him and he told me about an old book. I was dancing in a club there and he used to come in at night and I would sit at his table when I wasn't working. I didn't know him very well then and I asked what he was doing, and he said he was hunting for an old book."

"What book?"

"He didn't say. I thought it was a joke. Later he said he found the book and that it was going to be very valuable."

"Try and remember more," I said. It was nice sitting there watching her put on her makeup, watching the tiny movements of the muscles in her shoulders. The perfume she used made me think of my mother's garden. There was a bed of pinks in the garden and in the spring the air was heavy with the spicy smell of them.

"Once he said something about a map," Dorothy Allen said, half turning. There was mascara on her eyelashes now and they looked longer than ever. "Did he ever write you anything about a book or a map?"

"No," I said. "He wrote me about making a lot of money out of something, but that's all."

"Maybe it was the book. Sometimes old books are worth a lot, aren't they?"

"Sometimes. It depends what they are."

"I should have asked him. Only you don't ask Arthur things. You wait for him to tell you. And he never told me."

That was true enough, I knew. Arthur had always been reticent about his work and his plans. When he got ready to tell you, he lost his reticence. It did no good to ask him. I wondered if the book had any significance. It seemed improbable. In the first place, Arthur knew little about books, modern or ancient. In the second, the sort of old books one found in Mexico were, as a rule, valuable only to scholars. And maps? How could one make a fortune from a map? Probably she had misunderstood the enthusiasm of an archeologist. Values to them were relative. An old rock with carvings on it might seem priceless. A knock interrupted my musings. A voice told Miss Allen they were ready for her. I stood up.

"Good night," I said.

"Don't go, Mitchell."

"But you have to work."

"You get a table. I'll come and sit with you when I finish my number."

I said that would be fine and went back into the café. The waiter showed me all his teeth. The fact that I knew Miss Allen seemed to impress him. I ordered another beer and drank it slowly, thankful she had asked me to stay. I didn't want to go back to the room because I knew I wouldn't sleep. There were too many things to think about. Mostly there was Joe Briggs and I kept seeing him lying on the couch with the knife I had made in his back and I felt very much to blame for his death. If I hadn't written to him—but there was no use going back. I had written and he had been drawn into this case and now he was dead. I knew Arthur hadn't killed him. I knew also that his death and Arthur's disappearance were rooted in the same mysterious mire.

Dorothy Allen came out on the floor in front of the orchestra and the music started. There was nothing extraordinary about her dancing, but she was graceful and full of rhythm. Her feet tapped the polished floor as though it were a big drum and the soles of her little shoes were the sticks. I was watching her so closely that I didn't see Jacques Magnin until he was standing by my table. There was another man with him, a squat, fat-faced Mexican who smelled of perfume.

"I didn't expect to find you here," Magnin said with his curiously sweet smile.

"I didn't expect to find myself here." I motioned to a chair. "Sit down, won't you?"

"Thanks," Magnin said. "This is Raul Amaro, Dr. Drake."

The fat-faced Mexican bowed. "So pleased," he said. "Drake. You are the biographer, no?" He handled English easily though a little oddly. The words seemed to roll out of his mouth. I nodded and he flashed his teeth at me. "Your brother. He worked with me at Guadalajara."

"He mentioned you," I said.

My hand was pumped vigorously. Amaro sat down and kept on smiling. "Where is Arturo?"

"That's why I'm here," I said. "I don't know."

"No?"

"I'm trying to find him," I said.

"Strange." The smile went away. "Very strange. Ah, but he will appear."

The waiter's shadow fell on the table. We ordered drinks and he went away. "How small the world," Amaro said.

"I was thinking that," Magnin agreed. "Dr. Drake gives me letters. Then I meet him here. By the way, it wasn't necessary to use the letters. Mr. Amaro"—he gave his friend a warm smile—"we had met before in Lisbon. He has been very kind."

"It is nothing." Amaro dismissed the matter with a wave of his pudgy hand.

I thought of the book *Bloody Harvest* and wondered if Amaro had worked with Magnin in Lisbon. Then I wondered how Magnin would react to the news of the murder. I said, "You might as well tear up that note to Joe Briggs. Someone murdered him tonight."

Magnin pulled his eyebrows down and stared across the table at me.

"The journalist?" Amaro asked, and there was real concern in his voice.

"Yes."

"Oh no. A fine man. A fine honorable man. Murdered. It is impossible."

"It isn't," I said. "It happened. It happened tonight." As I told them about it, I regretted speaking. Relating what had occurred made me feel much worse.

"Incredible," Amaro said when I was silent. Magnin took a lump of sugar from the bowl and crumbled it in his long fingers, still not saying anything.

"But they will find his murderer." Amaro put a lot of

certainty into his tone. "Madero will find him. A very clever man, Madero."

"So I've heard," I said. I didn't want to talk about it any more. I wanted to get up and go out and walk very fast in the rain but there was the waiter with another beer for me and the drinks for my companions and right behind him was Dorothy Allen. We stood up.

"I liked the dance," I said.

She smiled.

"Please sit down," I said.

"You know each other too?" Amaro almost bubbled. "But of course. Arturo. Of course. Good evening, Miss Allen."

She took the chair beside me. I told the waiter to bring her a drink and then introduced Magnin. I didn't like the way he looked at her body. His eyes seemed to have hunger in them. I thought of Penny Gage and wished I had told her aunt that Magnin was in Mexico. "I suppose you know that Miss Gage will be here in a few days," I said.

"What?" Magnin was no longer staring at the dancer.

"They're driving down." I watched him and wondered how long he could hold his breath.

"When?"

"In a few days."

"They haven't started then?"

"I don't think so."

His sigh had relief in it or so it seemed to me. He took his gaze from my face and studied his knuckles. Suddenly I found myself disliking the man intensely. I wanted to reach across the table and push his nose a bit farther to the left. I knew it didn't make sense. I should be grateful that he didn't want Penny following him, that he was through with her.

"I think they plan to leave in a couple of days," I said.

"It will be nice seeing them." Magnin gave his attention back to Miss Allen. But not for long. He finished his brandy, looked at his watch and got up. "I must be going. If you don't mind."

I stood up and Amaro stood up. "Good night," I said. Magnin bowed. "Good night."

"I must go too," Amaro said. He picked up Miss Allen's hand and kissed it. I decided I didn't like him much either. I watched them go out and when I couldn't see them any more I felt relieved.

Miss Allen glanced at me oddly. "You upset him."

"Yes."

"Who is Miss Gage?"

I told her. I tried not to sound enthusiastic. I tried to make my interest purely academic. I wasn't successful.

"Are you in love with her?"

"Of course not," I said.

"Of course you aren't." She smiled impishly. "I've got to go back to work. Will I see you tomorrow?"

"Yes."

"Where can I reach you?"

I told her. She patted my hand. "I'm glad you're here, Mitchell."

"I am too," I said. That wasn't true. I remembered that Joe Briggs was dead and I was sure he would still be alive if I had stayed away. "Good night, Miss Allen."

"Dorothy."

"Good night, Dorothy."

"Good night, Mitchell. Things may be better tomorrow."

"They can't be much worse." I watched her cross the room and thought again how lovely her body was. Then I paid the check and went outside. It had stopped raining and above the dark street I could see stars.

It was two when I reached the hotel. The lobby was deserted. I nodded to the night clerk and he nodded back and came around and followed me into the elevator and ran it up for me. It creaked dismally.

I was glad I had left the light burning. Then the room didn't seem quite so lonely. I went in and shut the door and wished I was back in Mrs. Huntting's boarding house. And

51

I realized the reason I wanted to be back was Penny Gage. Well, she would be here soon. In a few days I would see her. I tried to take comfort from the thought. I remembered Magnin and how upset he had been and how he had hurried from the café. There had been something he wanted to do right away and I was pretty sure I knew what it was. I was sure he had hurried out to send a wire to Penny, a wire telling her to stay away from Mexico. Would it stop her? I doubted it. I sat on the bed and considered the matter for a while and realized I didn't want to stop Penny. Dorothy Allen's question rang in my ears—was I in love with her? Of course not, I had said. That wasn't the right answer. I tried to push her out of my thoughts. There was a murder to solve, a murder for which I was, in a measure, responsible. And there was Arthur. Yet here I sat worrying over a girl and my emotions regarding that girl. I saw Magnin's thin, sensitive face again. I remembered I had given him a letter to Joe Briggs. Was that significant? I put my head in my hands, closed my eyes and tried to think clearly but clarity wouldn't come. There was only a whirling, roaring confusion. So I got up presently and opened my bag to get my pajamas. Then I knew someone had been in my room. Someone had gone through my things again—someone who hadn't been too careful about it.

SIX

A BELLBOY who had spent two years driving a laundry truck around Brooklyn brought me a telegram at seven o'clock.

"Changed plans. Flying down. Arrive five P.M. tomorrow," the wire read. It was signed Molly Gage and it had been sent the night before.

I told the boy to bring me the papers and some coffee.

"American coffee?" he wanted to know.

"Café con leche," I said.

I took a shower and shaved and wondered how Magnin would react to the sudden appearance of the Gage menage.

52

I didn't think he would like it. After a while the boy came back with the papers and a tray with two pots on it and I sat on the bed and drank my coffee and read the accounts of Joe's murder. They told me little. He had been stabbed about five-thirty yesterday afternoon, and that's all anyone seemed to know. My name wasn't mentioned. Neither was Arthur's. Madero had found the body, the papers said. They didn't say why the detective had gone to Joe's apartment. They just said he had discovered the body and was working on the case. There were some long stories about Joe's life, and I was reading them when the clerk called and said John Aldrich was downstairs.

From his appearance I judged he had slept very little. He squeezed my arm, and said, "Hello, boy, let's have breakfast. I haven't eaten."

The dining room was on the fifth floor, so we didn't bother with the elevator. We walked up the marble stairs and out to the roof garden and took a table in the sun. It was a fine clear day and over the edge of the roof to the east you could see the tops of the two snow-covered mountains and there were clouds sitting on them.

"Madero came by last night," Aldrich said. "He's a clam."

"He's an Indian," I said.

"I was a clam too," Aldrich went on. "Told him damned little. A shrewd little devil. Probably three jumps ahead of us already. Did you see the dancer?"

I nodded. "No luck there."

"Didn't think there would be."

Then I remembered the book business. I repeated the conversation. Aldrich scowled, shook his head. "Can't make anything of it."

"Nor I."

"Just talk, probably. Unless—" He seemed to be studying the bill of fare. He wasn't. He was thinking, for presently he added: "Old books. Maps. Oh no. Couldn't be."

"What?"

"Fairy tales. Lost mines. Moctezuma's treasure. No, no."

"Definitely no, no," I said.

"Worth a thought anyway. Next time you go through his things it might be good to keep old books in mind."

"All right," I said and because the waiter was standing there looking nervous I gave him my order. Aldrich indicated that huevos rancheros was what he wanted too. I said: "What do you make of Joe's death?"

He shrugged. "Mexico."

"Meaning?"

"Violence. No regard for life. I'm getting too old for it, Mitchell."

"You're not old."

"Too old," Aldrich said. "Maybe he wrote something out of line."

"Not Joe."

"Even Joe."

"But why was he killed right now? No, John. It has something to do with Arthur. Something to do with my being here."

"Don't be too sure." Then he smiled kindly. "You're blaming yourself, boy. Don't do that."

"I'll try not to."

We ate and talked and moved in mental circles. But at least it was warm in the sun and fairly peaceful. Some of the noise of the street came up to the roof, but not too much. I was sorry when he said he had to go to the office. When you had someone to talk to, someone you knew, things seemed a little better. Well, I'd have someone to talk to soon enough. Madero. I went downstairs with Aldrich, bought a package of Monte Carlo cigarettes at the newsstand and returned to my room.

I didn't have to wait long. At eight-thirty the phone rang. There was a gentleman to see me. I didn't ask who the gentleman was. I guessed it was José Manuel Madero and the guess was right. I heard the elevator creaking as it rose slowly skyward, heard the door clang shut, heard footsteps outside and a light rap.

"Come in," I said.

Madero came in, closed the door and smiled. He wasn't in green today. His suit was blue and his tie was blue and his shirt was blue. He said, "Good morning," in a voice as bright as his costume.

"Nice of you to come to me," I said. "I expected a trip to the police station."

"There is no need to visit the police station yet." His "yet" sounded ominous. He sat, carefully pulled up his trousers, opened his cigarette case, flipped a cigarette out with his thumbnail and caught it in his mouth. He lit it and smiled at me through the smoke. Then he started asking questions.

There may be more thorough detectives than Madero. I doubt it. His method was to start at the beginning and go on from there. There were questions about Father and Mother, about Arthur, about Joe Briggs and John Aldrich. He wanted Arthur's history and my history. But I held a few things back during that two-hour inquisition. There was a good reason—Arthur.

If I hadn't been so upset, I might have enjoyed my session with Madero. He was gentle and sympathetic. Every now and then he apologized for taking up so much of my time. I kept thinking that here was a man I could trust. Then I reminded myself that he represented the law and that for some unknown reason the law was deeply concerned with my brother. If Joe hadn't been murdered, I might have taken a chance, might have told him everything.

Perhaps not.

Presently he shifted from the past to the present. Arthur's friends. Who were they?

I shrugged. "John Aldrich," I said. "The men he worked with at Guadalajara."

"I know them. Look, Dr. Drake. Come clean." He sounded like a New York policeman.

"I've come clean," I said.

"Your brother—you are certain you haven't seen him."

"No."

"And you haven't heard from him since October?"

"No."

"You can't tell me why Mr. Briggs was killed?"

"I wish I could. You know that as well as I. I liked Joe Briggs. I feel partly responsible for his death. I asked him to help me find my brother and he was murdered."

"Perhaps your brother does not wish to be found."

"That's ridiculous."

"Who knows?"

I leaned back against the bedstead feeling futile and helpless and for the first time a little angry with him. I said, "While you're here you might as well finish looking through my things."

"What do you mean finish?" His eyes were almost large.

"Maybe your man overlooked something last night."

"So you went out last night?"

"You know I went out."

"Where?"

"Walking," I said. "I couldn't stand the room so I walked."

"Of course."

"Go ahead." I pointed to my bags.

"There's no need, Dr. Drake. Thank you."

"Por nada," I said. "Now may I ask some questions?"

"Shoot." He made the word sound like a train whistle. It was incongruous, that word. Coming from him.

I asked questions until I felt like Clifton Fadiman. Certainly I had an expert on my hands, an expert at giving evasive answers when he wanted to. He wouldn't tell me why he wanted Arthur. He wouldn't tell me if he had anything definite on Joe's murder. All he would say was that Joe was stabbed at five-thirty, that whoever had done it had worn gloves, that no one had seen the murderer enter the apartment house. He was good enough to explain his theory of how it happened. "Someone was waiting for Mr. Briggs in the apartment," Madero said. "Standing so that when the door opened and admitted Mr. Briggs, the murderer was concealed. Then he stepped out and stabbed Mr. Briggs in the back and placed him on the couch."

"He?" I asked.

"Or she," Madero said. "A woman might have done it. I don't think Mr. Briggs knew who killed him."

"Any clues?"

He elevated his left shoulder. "When one wishes a murder kept secret, one leaves no trace."

"Except the knife," I said. "Have you traced that?" It was a question I had wanted to ask for a long time. One that I feared asking. If you knew the trick it was easy to establish the ownership of that weapon—a half twist to the left, a quarter twist back, then the blade slid out of the handle.

"Not yet."

"It shouldn't be hard," I said.

"Perhaps not."

"Do you think the knife's owner killed Joe?" I didn't look at him.

"What do you think?"

"I don't know."

"Nor I." He stood up. He wasn't smiling now. His eyes had a far away look in them and I wondered if he was going home to his knitting. "You have been very kind," he said in Spanish. "Thank you."

"For nothing," I said. Not until he was gone did it occur to me that he had seemed surprised when I mentioned the search of my things. Was it his man who had been in my room last night? And if not, who then? And why?

SEVEN

IF ARTHUR had been a tourist I would have known where to

look for him. I would have haunted Sanborn's café in the House of the Blue Tiles, and the Wells Fargo office, a block east of Sanborn's on Madero. That's where most visiting Americans got their mail. But Arthur wasn't a tourist. He had never liked Sanborn's. And he didn't get his mail care of Wells Fargo. I did. That's why I met the man with the angel face again.

After Madero's departure I went downstairs and caught a west-bound bus to the Monument to the Revolution, then walked over to the Street of the Crying Woman. There was someone following me, but it didn't matter. Madero knew Arthur's address and I guessed he had been through the house. I spent a couple of hours going over Arthur's belongings again, with no success. I even looked for old books. There were two or three around, but the only one I thought might be worth more than a dollar was one of the Elsie Dinsmore series that had belonged to Mother when she was a small child. I questioned Dolores and Pablo Guzman for half an hour but that helped not at all. The Señor had hired them. The Señor had showed them about the house and had given them instructions to watch the place. Then he had gone away. When had he employed them? November 7, Pablo thought it was. Yes, that was the day. Then they had not lived in the house with Señor Drake? No. The day they entered his employ he had departed.

I gave up. I told them to report to me if anyone wished to enter the house, then headed back for the hotel. On the way I stopped in at the Wells Fargo office for my mail.

As usual, there was a line in front of the mail window. It took me ten minutes to reach the cage and I discovered I could have saved the time. No one had written. I was on my way out when I almost collided with the angel-faced young man who called himself Paul.

"My God," Paul said. "Where did you drop from?"

"The same place you did."

"When I have words with the spik yonder I'll buy you a drink," Paul said. "Hang on."

He came back with a couple of letters in his hand, but he didn't read them. He put them in his pocket, took my arm and propelled me into the sunshine. "This is a hell of a place," he observed. "How long you been here?"

"Since yesterday. And you?"

"Three or four days. Too long."

"Don't you like it?"

"No." He was emphatic.

"It grows on you," I said.

"It won't grow on me," Paul said. "As soon as I wind up my chore, I'm heading back."

"But you'll return," I said. "They always do."

"Like Hawaii or Catalina," Paul said. "Nuts. Let's take a cab."

"Where?"

"The Reforma, Mister."

"Not on this street, then. It runs the wrong way."

"They all run the wrong way for me," Paul said.

We went north a block and I hailed a cab and bargained, in Mexican, with the driver. Paul looked impressed when the driver said it would cost seventy-five centavos.

"The thieves," he complained. "They've been sticking me a peso-fifty up. What you doing down here, Mister? Why aren't you riding herd on those dames?"

"Research," I said.

"I know a lot better places for research. That school for one."

"Not my type of research. And you?"

"I'm on a sort of diplomatic mission." He offered no explanation and I didn't ask for one. I was beginning to suspect that my two meetings with him might not be due entirely to coincidence. The man intrigued me. Whoever he was, I liked him, which was unusual for me. Ordinarily I'm not drawn to people at once. And whoever he was, he didn't have nerves of steel. The cab ride terrified him. That was understandable because we missed pedestrians by millimeters, jumped signals, tore across crowded streets and shot around corners. Paul took a deep breath when the cab stopped in front of the imposing bulk of the Reforma.

"Tell him how grateful we are," Paul said. "Why isn't everyone dead in this town?"

"They're a hardy people."

"Or they do not care about living." Paul paid the driver and we crossed the sidewalk. A boy tried to sell us lottery tickets. A little girl asked for money. Two men wanted to shine our shoes. And on the stairs a boy gave us a quick look at some postcards in the cup of his grimy fist. I remembered climbing the Pyramid of the Sun once late in the afternoon when there didn't seem to be anyone within ten miles and finding two urchins waiting for me at the top with baskets of stone images. That was Mexico for you.

It was cool and dark in the taproom. There were two elderly women at the center table drinking daiquiris and writing postcards and a group of well-dressed men at another who were talking in loud voices about a party that had lasted two days. We went over to a corner table and told the waiter to bring us beer.

"I don't know your last name," I said.

"Brent. Paul Brent."

"Odd we should meet down here, isn't it?"

"That's life," Paul said. "What do you do in this town if you don't like night clubs or hand ball or movies or churches?"

"On Sundays there are bull fights."

He made a face. "I saw one once in Tia Juana. That was enough. A mean, cruel lot, the Mexicans. They kick their dogs and beat their burros and stick knives in bulls. They go along the streets lugging coffins."

"They're fatalists."

"I'm a fatalist," Paul said. "But you don't see me packing my old man's coffin down the boulevard." He drank half his beer as though to wash the memory of things he had seen away. "What sort of research are you up to, Mister?"

I didn't look at him. I held my glass in both hands and stared at the amber liquid. No coincidence, I thought. Well there was only one thing to do and that was find out what he wanted from me. It might help. I said, "I'm down here looking for my brother."

His gaze was on my face. I looked up and saw how cold his eyes were. Almost the color of obsidian. "What's happened to him?"

"I don't know. He's disappeared. I'm trying to find him."

"When did he come down?"

"He lives here." I told him a little about Arthur and now I was watching his face. But all I could see in his expression was friendly concern. Maybe I was wrong. Maybe it was coincidence after all. Such things did happen.

"Damned funny, isn't it? How about the cops? Have you asked them to help?"

"No. There's no need. They're already looking for him."

"Oh oh," Paul said. "There's your answer. I wouldn't worry too much. If the cops were looking for me, I wouldn't be found either. Even by my brother, Mister. Maybe he hates cops."

"I've another reason to worry," I said, still watching him closely. "I'm mixed up in a murder."

Paul whistled. "Here?"

"Yes. A friend was helping me. I went to see him last night. Someone murdered him."

"That one." Paul sat very straight. "I read about it this morning." He flicked his glass with his forefinger, sucked air in through his closed teeth. "But they didn't mention you."

"No."

"Then beat it. Get out of this town. That's what I'd do."

"No use."

"Want 'em to pin it on you?"

"They won't do that."

"The hell they won't."

"They know I was there," I said. "There are little men following me around."

A startled look crossed his face. He glanced over his shoulder at the door.

"Outside, probably," I said. "Waiting."

He signaled to the waiter. "A double Canadian club. You better have one."

"I'll stick to beer."

"You look like such a shy guy, too," Paul said.

"You may have company now," I said.

"Me?"

"Yes. My little man will pass the word on that you were with me and then they'll start following you around."

"That will be fine."

"Do you mind?"

"Oh no. It will keep me from getting lonesome."

I thought he was lying. I thought he minded very much from the look in his eyes. "I hope it doesn't interfere with your diplomatic work," I said.

"I hope so too. Let's not worry about me. I haven't any brother and I didn't walk in on a guy with a shiv in his back. Any women mixed up in this?"

"No," I lied.

"Who knocked off your friend? Any idea?"

I shook my head.

"Give me the works, Mister."

"I have."

"I wear long pants," Paul said. "I'm dry behind the ears. You tell me your brother stops writing to you and you come down to look for him. So you get a newspaper guy to help you and he is knocked off. I ask you. That isn't all. Who else is in on it?"

Who else? That was a question I couldn't answer. Dorothy Allen, John Aldrich, Ruiz, Amaro, Magnin? They might fit into the picture but I didn't see how. I said, "I don't know."

He swallowed his drink, said, "Nuts."

"I really don't."

"And you don't know what your brother was up to?"

"No."

"Those aren't little men following you around," Paul said. "They are birds. They are waiting to cover you with leaves. Either that or you're a liar."

"Maybe we're both liars," I said.

He laughed. "Where you staying?"

"The Ontario."

"I'm here," Paul said. "If you need me."

We went upstairs and through the lobby that was so thoroughly American you couldn't tell Mexico was just outside the door. "So long," Paul said. "I'll look you up before I leave town."

"Do that," I said, and left him.

EIGHT

THAT AFTERNOON, while I waited for the plane, I tried very hard to find a place for Paul Brent in the murder picture. It couldn't be done. For that matter, there wasn't any picture. Just a blurred flat surface. I was glad I had gone for the mail. Otherwise I might have missed him and then Madero would have missed him too. Now he was Madero's problem as well as mine and if he was involved in Joe's murder, the detective would find out. It seemed to me the only way of finding Joe's murderer and getting to the heart of the mystery of my brother's disappearance was to blunder ahead and let things happen until something turned up you could grasp and hold. If I hadn't been so distraught I might have patted myself on the back for the Brent interview. I had given him something to think about—perhaps a rope with which to hang himself. At least, that's what I thought as I stood in the late afternoon sunshine and looked, now and then, toward the north. There was little wind but what there was was dust-laden, for it came across the lake bed. I remembered when the lake had amounted to something, but that was a long time ago. Now it was nearly dry and in time would be drier. It seemed almost unbelievable that five centuries ago the water had been deep where I was now standing and that on its surface the boats of the Aztecs moved from Texcoco to Tenochitlan, on whose ruins the capital had risen.

East, the mountains rose, but you couldn't see the tops for the clouds. Occasionally a small plane circled and it was hard to tell it from one of the ever-present buzzards wheeling overhead. I looked at my watch. It was almost five-thirty. Then I realized I was excited, that the day had suddenly become bright.

Things began to happen around the airport. Men came out wheeling carts and groups of people swarmed up to the fence. I saw the plane coming in and felt breathless and young. It circled once, then slid down and taxied across, sun flashing from its silver wings and from its whirling propellers. Then it stopped and men pushed a platform up to the door and opened the door and a moment later I saw her. Her aunt was right behind.

They came toward me. Penny was looking around as though searching for someone and then the good feeling went away. I had forgotten Magnin. Well, he wasn't here; I was certain of that. She'd have to wait to see him.

Molly Gage smiled, held out her hand. She greeted me as though she hadn't seen me for years. That's how distance affects you. It makes you forget time.

"Hello, Mitchell," she said gaily.

I tried to be cheerful. "I haven't changed," I said. "You two haven't changed either."

"Good of you to meet us, Dr. Drake," Penny said. As we shook hands she kept looking past me and then her gaze met mine and I knew she wanted to know about him.

I wanted sympathy. I wanted to pour my troubles out to Molly Gage, but I didn't. I said nothing about Joe or about Arthur on the drive into the city. I pointed out churches. I told them the history of the streets along which we passed. Penny's eyes were bright with excitement and I tried to tell myself she was excited at seeing new places and new people. I knew better.

Not until they were settled in their suite at the Hotel Reforma did Penny have an opportunity to speak to me alone. I had left them there, promising to meet them at eight for dinner and was waiting for the elevator when Penny came out of her room and hurried after me. She got into the elevator and I could see she wanted to ask questions and I could see also that she hated to ask them.

"I'm going to walk," Penny said. "Would you like to walk with me?"

"I'd be glad to."

"You're sure you haven't anything else to do?"

"I'm sure."

It was dusk and the lights were coming on. A cool wind had risen and we walked fast along Reforma toward the city, not speaking at first, and I tried not to think of Magnin or Joe or my brother, tried only to take pleasure from the moment, from her presence at my side.

"It's nice having you here," I said after a while.

"It's nice being here," Penny said. "I want to telephone. Will you take me where there's a telephone?"

"There are phones in the hotel."

"I know it. I didn't want to call from there."

Across the boulevard there was a café. I led her through the stream of traffic to the other side and we went in. A plump woman with a rose behind her ear pointed to a hallway when I asked where the telephone was and Penny went down the hall. I could hear her giving central the number in halting Spanish. When she came back a moment later she seemed ready to cry.

"He's moved," she said. "They don't know where he moved to."

"That's too bad."

"I wired him last night we were coming," Penny said. "This morning he moved."

"Perhaps he didn't get the wire," I said. "This is Mexico and sometimes the service is bad."

"I've got to find him."

"We'll find him," I said. "Don't worry about it." I could have told her about Magnin's reaction the night before, but I didn't. I could have told her that his sudden departure from the place he was living was the result of her wire, but I didn't. I knew that would hurt her and I didn't want to hurt her.

"Could my telegram have missed him?" She put her hand on my arm.

"Certainly," I said. "You better go back to your aunt. She'll worry about you."

"Have you seen him?"

"No," I said.

"Maybe—" Her eyes seemed to have fear in them and she put her hand up to her lips, but she didn't finish the sentence.

"Maybe what?"

"Nothing," Penny said and led the way out of the café. We walked back to the hotel in silence. In the lobby as we waited for an elevator I saw Paul Brent lounging near the desk. He saluted and I could see he was examining Penny with interest. I didn't blame him. I felt a sudden foolish pride at standing there with her.

"Eight o'clock," I said, when the elevator doors opened. "And don't worry too much. I might be able to find him for you."

"Really?" Her face brightened. "Where?"

"A couple of places."

"Would you take me?"

"We'll see," I said. The doors closed and she was gone. Brent spoke as I passed him. "Fast work, Mister."

I realized what he meant. He thought Penny was someone I had picked up. "She's an old friend," I said a little coldly.

Paul Brent grinned.

NINE

IT WAS after seven when I started for the Reforma Hotel. I went along Tacuba until it became Hidalgo—streets in Mexico City have an odd habit of becoming something else— and along Hidalgo to the park and then across the park in the cool dusk. It was nearly eight when I climbed the Reforma steps. Penny and her aunt were waiting for me in the lobby.

We had dinner at the Tacuba where the food was good and where a peso was a peso, not one-fifth of a dollar. Arthur and I used to eat there a good deal before I went away and the woman at the cashier's desk remembered me. Afterwards we took Penny's aunt back to the hotel.

"Sorry I can't go with you," Molly Gage said. "Some other night."

"I'm sorry too," I said. I wondered where we were supposed to be going, but I didn't ask.

"I know you'll take good care of her."

"Of course."

"Do they often have fiestas at night?"

"Not very often."

"This is a special one," Penny put in. "They only have it the night Juan Diego saw the Virgin of Guadalupe."

"That's a lovely myth, isn't it," Molly Gage said.

"I always liked it." I gave Penny what I hoped was a reproving look.

"I'm sorry," she said when her aunt was safe in the elevator. "It was the only think I could think of."

"When did Juan Diego see the Virgin?"

"In January," Penny said. "In 1531."

"This is February. And it wasn't at night."

"Stop being a professor."

I forgot for the moment Penny's reason for tampering with miracles. She wasn't one of my students. She was a lovely young woman full of warmth and laughter. She brought me back to earth with a question. "Do you really think you can find him?"

"I can't promise. I can try."

"You saw him. You said you didn't, but I think you did." There were tiny smile wrinkles at the corners of her eyes.

"No."

"You're blushing. You shouldn't lie. You can't do it properly. Why don't you want me to see him?"

"I don't—well, I don't approve of him."

"Neither does Aunt Molly."

"You're young," I said.

"So is he."

"All right," I said. "He's young and he's fascinating and he has suffered. Suppose we let it go at that."

"You don't like him."

"I don't know him."

"Why don't you like him? Is it because—" She didn't finish the sentence. Her glance had mischief in it. "I think it is," she added.

"What?"

"Never mind. Come on." She linked arms and we went through the lobby. I left Penny in a big chair and ferreted out a telephone. I found Amaro's name in the book and called him, but he wasn't in. I called Ruiz on the chance he might have seen Amaro, but he was out too. I decided they might be at the El Toro. If not, it didn't matter. In fact, I hoped there would be no one around who could tell us where Mr. Magnin was. A momentary feeling of guilt—of betrayal—seized me. I should be trying to find out who killed Joe—trying to find my brother—and here I was wasting time because I wanted to be near Penny Gage. Then I eased my conscience by thinking that Magnin might be one of the keys to the puzzle.

It was ten o'clock when we left the hotel. I said it was too early to start searching. It wasn't true. I wanted to be alone with her a while longer. We found a cab and I told the driver to take us out Reforma Boulevard and through Chapultepec Park. I glanced back two or three times. No one seemed to be following us, but it was hard to tell because of the traffic. I wondered if Madero had decided to take me off the list.

The night was warm and clear and there were a great many young men and women sitting under the trees with their arms around each other. I told the driver to wait and we got out and walked along a path through the trees and above us we could see the half moon riding on its back.

"Some night we'll go to Xochimilco," I said. "Some night when the moon is full."

Penny looked up at me. "That will be fine." There was a curious note in her voice.

"I haven't been there for years," I said. "A long time ago I used to go out there at night and get a boat and lie back looking at the moon."

"Alone?"

"Not always."

"You know you're—" She hesitated.

"I'm what."

"Not at all like you were in school."

"I was supposed to be a teacher."

"Maybe it's Mexico," Penny said.

"Maybe."

"I was always a little afraid of you. I'm not any more. You seem like a—well—more human."

"There's no platform to stand on. You can't look up to me."

"Oh but I can." We were facing each other and she tilted her head and smiled. The moonlight put a shadow of a branch across her lips and it seemed to me there was the reflection of stars in her eyes. "It's odd, isn't it?" she went on. "How you feel about people. How you take them and make them part of your lives. Did you know I made you part of my life?"

"Along with Magnin."

"No, no. I didn't know it either until there was no more school and you had gone."

I laughed. "You'll be telling me next you came down here to see me."

"Don't make fun of me."

"I won't, child."

"I'm not a child."

"Come on," I said and led the way back to the cab.

Magnin wasn't at the El Toro. Nor was Ruiz nor Amaro. Dorothy Allen was dancing and when she finished she came over to our table. "Hello, Mitchell." She sat down beside me and put her hand on my shoulder. I introduced them. Penny looked at Dorothy and then she looked at me.

"Mitchell's my new brother," Dorothy said. The imp was back in her eyes.

"That's nice," Penny said.

I realized I hadn't told Penny about Dorothy and Arthur but this didn't seem a propitious time. I wondered if Penny would understand the dancer's possessive attitude. I did. Arthur was my brother and she loved Arthur and it was quite natural for her to think of me as part of her family. Nevertheless, I felt a little uncomfortable, so I asked if Magnin or Amaro had been in.

"The men who were here last night?"

Penny flashed a look at me. She nodded her head but she didn't speak.

"Yes," I said.

"No. Are you going to buy me a drink?" Dorothy asked. I beckoned to the waiter. "Brandy," Dorothy ordered.

"I'll have a brandy too," Penny said.

I thought about Penny's aunt and I wanted to say I thought one brandy in an evening was enough, but decided not to. "Three," I told the waiter.

When the brandy came we drank it and talked about Mexico

and then Dorothy left us to change her costume. "She has a lovely figure," Penny observed. "Don't you think so?"

"Yes."

"She thinks so too."

"She's a dancer."

"I forgot you were her new brother."

"I'm not. Not yet."

"Shall I write home and tell the class about your new sister?"

I was glad the waiter came up at that moment. "Another brandy," Penny said.

"You've had enough."

"I'm nineteen. I drink brandy at home."

"Not three in a row."

"Stop being stuffy."

"I'm being sensible." I frowned at her. "Now look here. Your aunt—"

"Thinks Dr. Drake is perfect," Penny said. "Shall I tell Aunt Molly about your new sister?"

"I don't care what you tell her."

"I'm teasing." She was smiling now. "Because you lied to me. Why did you lie to me?"

"I didn't intend to."

"How was he?"

"All right. I saw him only for a moment. Just to nod."

"I don't believe that either," Penny said. "I'll be good. But I like to see you blush. You don't seem old at all when you blush. I really think it's nice you have a new sister."

I gave the waiter a five-peso note. "Nothing more." I stood up. "It's time we were home."

"Aren't you going to tell her good-by?"

"I'll see her later."

"I'm not surprised."

"Let's go," I said. I must have spoken angrily because Penny stopped smiling and followed me out. The street was deserted. I took her arm and we walked toward Juarez and we were half a block away from the El Toro when she spoke. "I'm sorry. Don't be angry."

"I'm not."

"Yes, you are."

"No," I said. I wasn't. I was suddenly depressed. For a little while I had pushed my troubles aside, had forgotten about Arthur and Joe. That's what her upturned face with the moonlight on it had done to me. That's what the touch of her hand had done to me.

"Let's walk." Penny's fingers curled themselves around my arm. We turned west on Juarez. Over Chapultepec Heights the moon was riding. The wind was dry and cool.

It was early yet, not midnight; but the city was quiet. Changed, I thought. In the old days at this time it was noisy and lively and it wasn't unusual to hear someone blazing away with a pistol. Even the Regis Hotel, where once the generals and politicians spent their nights figuring out ways to loot the country, was quiet. Everyone in the place seemed to have gone to bed. I wondered if Ruiz was in bed. I wondered if Ruiz had any part in what had happened. No use wondering. I said, "Tomorrow I'll do it."

"What?" Her fingers were warm on my arm.

"Find him for you."

"Oh," Penny said.

"Amaro will know where he is."

"Yes," Penny said.

Again we were silent, walking close together along the almost deserted street. Perhaps it was the night, so peaceful it robbed one's senses of the feel of danger; perhaps it was the presence of Penny Gage; perhaps it was the burden of trouble on my mind. Anyway, I had no foreboding of what happened then. They were on us suddenly. One moment we were alone, passing the statue of Charles IV, which the Mexican affectionately calls the Horse. The next, three men were on us.

"Run, Penny," I yelled and started lashing out with both

fists. One man went down and his hands grasped my leg. I kicked him and was free. Something hit my cheek and I reeled away, then straightened and grappled with a stocky man. My fingers closed around his throat and I shook him and tried to force him down. Something crashed against my skull. I heard a woman scream; I heard a shot, and then there was darkness all around me.

TEN

A VOICE said in Mexican, "He is not dead." I struggled up through the roaring darkness toward the voice and for a minute I was a little boy again. Arthur and I were riding a burro along a rocky trail and the burro shied at a bit of paper and I fell off. I said thickly, "I'm all right, Art."

"Mitchell," and I knew it was Penny's voice. "Oh, Mitchell."

I remembered what had happened. I opened my eyes and there was Penny bending over me, and beside her was Paul Brent. Near him half a dozen Mexicans smoked cigarettes unexcitedly.

"Come on, Mister," Paul said. "We've got to get out of here."

Penny was stroking my forehead and I didn't want to get up. I wanted to lie there on the pavement with my eyes closed and feel the softness of her hand on my forehead.

Brent's voice was sharp. "Get up. We've got to beat it before the cops come."

They helped me to my feet and I shook my head and then I could see clearly. I could see the Horse and a few faint stars and the moon.

"I thought you were killed," Penny said. She was holding my left arm with both hands.

"I thought so too," I said. "What happened?"

"They ran," Paul said dryly. "Come on now."

There was a cab parked by the curb and we climbed in and one of the Mexicans threw away his cigarette and got under the wheel. "Hotel Reforma," Paul told him.

"Does it hurt awfully?" Penny asked.

"Not much," I said but I let her hold my hand.

"It was a good thing I was following you," Paul observed. "Those boys seemed bent on mischief. But they didn't like firearms."

"I thought I heard a shot."

"That was me. I missed."

"What were you following us for?" Penny turned and stared at Brent.

"Dough," Paul said succinctly. "Here we are. How do you tell one of these babies to forget something?" He gave the driver five pesos. I spoke to the man in Mexican, he nodded, grinned, and drove away.

"We'll have a drink." Paul led the way to the tap-room. "You look like you need one, Professor."

I needed one all right. My head ached horribly and I was still a bit confused. I sat down and put my hand over my eyes.

"Are you sure you're all right?" Penny's voice was like a cool cloth on my aching forehead.

"I'm fine."

"One of 'em laid a blackjack across your skull," Brent explained. "Don't you know any better? You get yourself mixed up in a murder and then you go wandering around the streets at midnight."

"Murder?" Penny's blue eyes were bigger than ever. "You didn't—"

"No, I didn't," I said. "I saw no need to worry you."

"Who?"

"A friend. A newspaperman." I explained about Arthur and about coming down to search for Arthur and about Joe being killed.

"Oh, Mitchell." Again she used my first name. "I was so

selfish. I bothered you with my own little worries." There was fear in her tone. "Those men. Were they trying to kill you too?"

"They were trying to do something," Paul said. "They weren't playing."

She frowned at him. "Were you following Mitchell?"

"No. You." The drinks had come and he paid for them and waved the waiter away. "I've been following you for quite a while."

"Oh. Then it was you—in Woodland—" She left the sentence unfinished.

"It was me. I was hired to keep an eye on you."

Concern became anger. Her eyes flashed and she bit her under lip. Then she started to get up.

"Now look, my girl," Paul said. "You're not supposed to know about this. I told you because you would have guessed anyway. I couldn't be Johnny-on-the-spot for no reason, could I? So don't go running to your aunt. That would get me fired and you packed back home."

So he was a private detective. Remembering my awkward attempt to draw him out, I felt foolish. I should have known. Molly Gage was no one's fool. She had seen through the Mexican trip.

"You gave me a time tonight," Paul went on. "I almost lost you in the park. Your friend"—he nodded at me— "did. And he lost me too. He was tailing us when we hit the park and then we shook him. Which was too bad, in a way. We could have used him back there."

The angry look left Penny's face. She was puzzled now, puzzled and a little afraid. She stared at Brent and then she stared at me. I said, "It's all right. There's nothing to worry about."

"Not a thing," Paul said ironically. "What have you got that they want?"

I shrugged. "I'm completely in the dark."

"Maybe you are," Paul said. "I didn't believe you this afternoon, but now I'm beginning to. Maybe I better start watching you too."

"Madero will take care of that."

"He didn't do such a good job of it tonight. Look, Mister. I'm supposed to be a detective. Give me the works."

I hesitated. Paul took a cardcase from his pocket, removed a card, put it in front of me. In the left hand corner was his name. In the center, in heavy letters, was printed: "Argosy Detective Agency."

"Miss Gage," Paul went on, "asked the agency to put someone on the child's tail. I'm it."

"Did she say why?" Penny asked. She was blushing, confused.

Brent nodded. "A guy. Now don't get sore. You can't blame her for wanting to keep an eye on you."

I looked at Penny and agreed with Paul Brent. I wanted to keep an eye on her too, only it seemed I wasn't the right person. Because of me, she had been in grave danger. And thinking of the midnight attack and the murder I began to wonder if everyone who associated with me was destined for trouble.

"The works," Brent insisted. "Spill it, Mister."

So I told him. I left nothing out. I went into my mind and found everything that seemed to have some bearing on the case—the letters from my brother and from Aldrich and from Joe and from Ruiz—Magnin's visit—Dorothy Allen—and the knife I had made, the knife that had robbed Joe Briggs of his life. Paul Brent sat there warming his glass in his hands and frowning at the table. Penny never took her eyes off my face and in them was a look of compassion that was warming and comforting.

She interrupted me once. She said, "You don't think that Jacques—?" and then she stopped.

"I don't know," I said. "I don't know anything."

"Jacques?" Paul asked.

"Magnin."

"He's the guy that got me hired," Paul said. "The writer."

I nodded. Penny stopped looking at me. She was examining her folded hands.

"Where's he now?" Paul asked.

I said I didn't know. I said we had gone to the El Toro looking for him.

"He's a good guy to stay away from," Brent said. Then he smiled at Penny. "Sorry, Miss Gage." Penny made no reply.

"What do you think of it?" I asked.

"It doesn't add up." Brent was thoughtful. "At least I can't add it. How about this Aldrich?"

"I've known him since I was a boy. He was my father's lawyer."

"Do you trust him?"

"Yes. I see no reason not to."

"Were he and your brother mixed up in any sort of a deal?"

"I don't know."

"Ruiz? Who's he?"

"He worked with Arthur at Guadalajara. They lived in the same house. I don't know much about him. Arthur liked him. He was fired from the Bureau of Anthropology when the new man took over."

"What's Ruiz do now?"

"I don't know that."

"And Amaro. How about him?"

"I know even less about Amaro. Arthur mentioned his name. That's all. I met him night before last with Magnin."

"Magnin and Amaro were together?"

I nodded. "They had met before. In Lisbon some years back. I don't know what they were doing in Lisbon. I can guess what Magnin was doing."

"Raising hell," Paul said dryly. "And the Allen dame?"

"You have all I know about her."

Brent sent smoke rings toward me. "Looks like your brother got himself mixed up with a bunch of trouble makers," he said thoughtfully. "That's how it seems to me. That would explain why the law was after him."

"Then the law would be after the others too," I said.

"Perhaps it is. Maybe Madero has his eye on them. But they stick around. Your brother doesn't. He scrams."

"And Joe?" I asked.

"Suppose Joe got wind of what they were up to?"

"No," I said. "Joe was murdered after I came to town. My being here has a great deal to do with it."

"It looks like it."

"What next?"

He shrugged.

"Should I tell Madero everything?"

"Depends on how much you think of your brother, Mister."

"Arthur had nothing to do with Joe's murder," I said.

"Maybe he couldn't help himself, Mister."

Penny spoke and though she made a flat statement her tone put a question in it. "Jacques had nothing to do with this. I'm sure."

"What's he hiding out for?" Paul asked.

"He isn't hiding out."

"He moved, didn't he?"

Penny studied the table top. She spoke without looking up. "He's afraid. He's afraid someone is going to kill him. That's why he didn't want me to come to Mexico."

"Kill him?" Brent sounded incredulous. "What for?"

"His book," Penny explained. "The things he told about in his book."

"I haven't read it," Paul said.

"He was a Communist," I explained. "An organizer first. Then a saboteur. He had a change of heart and went to confessional. Put it all on paper."

"Who'd kill him?"

"His boys. Or the ones he kicked around when he was on top."

"You really think so?"

78

"It has happened before. They have long memories." I looked at my watch. It was half past one. "The fiesta's over. You should be in bed." I smiled at Penny.

She didn't return the smile. She was tearing her paper napkin into little bits. Magnin, I thought. Worrying about him. And he wasn't worth it, that was the trouble. But there was nothing I could do—nothing anyone could do. She was young and her eyes put a romantic aura around the ex-revolutionary. There was no doubting his heroic stature if all he had written could be believed. For his beliefs he had gone through fire; had suffered awful torture; had risked death innumerable times. Then, bitter and disillusioned, turned on by the cause to which he had dedicated his life, he had told his story. You couldn't blame Penny for seeing in him a certain greatness of spirit, an indomitable courage.

"See you both tomorrow," Paul said when we reached the lobby. "Take a cab home, Mister."

I said I would.

"And if you want to see that guy, maybe I can help you find him," Paul told Penny. "I'm pretty good at finding people when I know where to look."

She gave him a faint smile, squeezed my arm and stepped into the elevator. The door closed and she was gone.

"There's a woman for you," Brent said. "Doesn't know what she wants."

"She knows," I said.

"No," Brent said. He stood on the porch watching me until I got into the cab, then he waved good night and went back into the hotel.

All the way to the Ontario I kept looking back and wondering if my three assailants were still on my trail. Apparently they weren't. I got out of the cab and went inside and up to my room and there was no one waiting for me in the room. But there was a note shoved under my door.

It was signed José Manuel Madero and it was so beautifully written it might have been engraved.

Dr. Drake. Tomorrow morning, at ten, if you have recovered sufficiently from your injuries would you call at my home. The address is Av. 916 Alva Ixtlixochitl.

ELEVEN

SEÑORA MADERO was not an Indian. And to judge from the pictures in the living room she was a Catholic. The pictures were very religious and looked a good deal like those you see on Mexican calendars. The memory of Carlotta lay heavily on the furnishings. Seeing the room and the plump, white-skinned Spanish woman surrounded by her treasures, I realized that the astute and taciturn detective was, before anything else, a husband. He might be an agnostic, he might work for a government that looked down its nose at the Church, but he let his wife worship as she pleased.

At first, when she opened the door for me and ushered me along a hall into the blue and plush and gilt of the high-ceilinged room, I thought Madero's wife was a mute. She wasn't. She spoke no English and took it for granted that being an American Spanish was unintelligible to me. Her eyes were magnificent. With eyes as large and as brown as those, one didn't need linguistic ability. And when Madero came into the room she oozed pride.

If I had expected pajamas and hurraches, I was disappointed. Madero was dapper as usual, in brown gabardine this time, with a yellow tie, a very yellow tie. He gave me a stiff little bow and said good day.

The discovery that I spoke her language seemed to delight Señora Madero. She beamed and was suddenly voluble. Madero let her talk, which was surprising. In Mexico, wives are often part of the furniture—little more important than the velvet drapes or the flowered carpets or the heavy plush bottomed chairs. You could see he believed in the emancipation of womanhood. Later I was to discover that every time he saw a woman plodding through the hills with a load on her back, it depressed him horribly. Presently she remembered I was a guest and offered me brandy, which I refused. Then she offered coffee.

"Thank you," I said.

"In the garden," Madero said. She bustled off and he led me down a hall and through a door into the sun-filled patio. There were flowers banked against the old walls and a pool with an arsenical-green frog sitting in the center of it. It reminded me of the frog in the Alameda which the shine boys painted every few years. As always, when I saw anything painted that awful green I wondered what there was about the color that appealed to the Mexican. We sat at an iron table and when Señora Madero brought a tray we drank café con leche and ate pan dulce and talked about the expropriation of the haciendas. Then Madero motioned to his wife. She smiled and withdrew.

"She calls me William Powell," Madero said fondly. "She is a movie fan." A smile covered his brown face. "An odd language, isn't it? A fan is something to cool you. Then it is an enthusiast." He spoke English now his wife was gone. "How is the head?"

"Fine." It wasn't. It ached a little and there was a lump at the base of the skull.

"You should eschew street brawls."

"Ordinarily I do."

"So far we have been unable to locate the men."

"I didn't see you around," I said. "I didn't see any of your men around."

"No. They were careless last night."

"How did you know then?"

"There was a report of a shooting at the Horse. A witness told of a thin American with glasses and a pretty girl and another American, a man with the face of an angel. Simple. You were seen with the angel-faced one yesterday. You met the girl at the airport."

"If you want the reason for the attack, I don't know it."

"This is why I asked you to call." He put his hand inside his jacket and brought out a package and there was no need for him to unwrap it. I knew what was inside. I knew without watching him put the slim parcel on the table and pull the paper off. It was the knife I had made for my brother.

"A child might have made it," Madero said softly. "Crude. But effective." He put his thumb against the needle-sharp piece of stone. "So many lives it has taken. Sacrifices, every one. Even Mr. Briggs, I think." He lit a cigarette, looked at me with half-closed eyes. "You recognize it?"

I made no reply.

"It was your brother's." It was a statement, not a question.

"How do you know?"

"Dr. Guittierez," Madero said. "The former head of the bureau which employed your brother. I showed it to him yesterday. A child did make the knife. You were the child."

"Yes," I said. "But my brother didn't kill Joe."

He raised his shoulders. I looked at his impassive, almost expressionless face and wanted to yell my belief in Arthur's innocence. But I knew it was futile. I waited.

"You are a scholar," Madero went on. "You have followed the bloody road that is the history of Mexico. You are, I think" —he used a Spanish word—"simpático. Your biography of Zapata." He flicked a bit of lint off his sleeve. "The work of a lover of freedom, that book. But your brother—" He let the sentence trail off with the smoke of his cigarette.

"A lover of freedom too," I said.

"Are you sure?"

"Yes."

"Did you ever hear of the 'Sons of Cortez'?"

I shook my head.

"I won't call it Fascist or Nazi," Madero explained. "Rather, it is what its name implies. The Spaniards took the land from us. We have taken it back. Now a group of men would take it from us again. The old order. The whip and the gun and the sword. The order against which Zapata and Hidalgo and Juarez fought. The Indian again under the heel. It is a rapidly growing organization, Dr. Drake. Not strong yet. But it can well be. We are seeking its leader. That is why we are seeking your brother."

"No," I said hotly. I stood up. "No. Not Arthur."

Madero's voice was gently monotonous. "In the basement of the house next to the one in which your brother lived in Gudalajara we found a printing press. It was on that press that the literature of the organization was printed. The press was purchased by Arthur Drake."

"Are you certain?"

"It was shipped from Chicago to your brother at Guadalajara. It was paid for with an American Express money order secured here by a man who said his name was Arthur Drake."

"Someone could have used his name." I tried not to shout.

"Possible, yes."

"And there were others living with him in Guadalajara. Ruiz and Amaro lived there."

"And another, Groz. He lived there too. They are all being investigated, Dr. Drake."

"What do they say?"

"Nothing," Madero said. "They have not been questioned. You see, the time is not yet to question them. We are waiting. The press remains in its hiding place." He crushed out his cigarette, started to throw it on the stones, then walked over to the brazier by the kitchen door and dropped it in the charcoal bucket. He smiled and sat down again. "Your brother may be innocent. The press may have been purchased by another, as you say. But we must find him and question him. Is that not logical?"

"Yes," I agreed.

"We are waiting to find the leader," Madero said. "Then we move."

I was fearful now, not because of the threat in that last statement but because I knew Mexico, knew the cruelty and ruthlessness and passion of revolution. One life, a thousand. Nothing. Death and the buzzards black against the sky. Arthur. Was he too one of its victims? I tried to be calm. I asked, "When was the printing press bought?"

"In December a year ago. Your brother was away from Guadalajara at the time."

"He came here?"

"Here and Vera Cruz," Madero said.

"Was he in Guadalajara when the press was delivered?"

"We are not sure."

"He might have been away?"

"He might have. He made several field trips during the next two months."

I wanted to call Madero a fool. Stupid, stupid. But he didn't know Arthur, couldn't know him as I did. To link him with an organization whose purpose was to grind down the peons again was puerile. Had Madero not mentioned the "Sons of Cortez" I might have told him everything I knew, for I was beginning to trust him. Now, full of anger, I was determined to make him fight for every crumb of information, to make him drag from me if he could anything I might know that would help him. It was a pig-headed attitude to take, but I was desperate and bitter and it seemed to me that the little man was looking no farther than the flat tip of his brown nose. I said, "It seems to me you are jumping at conclusions."

"Let us be the judge of that, Dr. Drake."

"My brother had nothing to do with the Sons of Cortez," I insisted. "You can be sure of that. He had nothing to do with Joe Briggs' murder. As soon as I find him, I'll prove it." And then I thought—find him, find him. Where was he? I tried to push back the feeling that I would never see him again. Not that, I thought. No, it couldn't be. He's alive. He'll return.

"I hope so," Madero said. "You see, I admire his brother very much. That is why I've told his brother so much that should not have been told."

"Thanks."

"And no one else must know it. No one, Dr. Drake."

"I think my attorney should know it. I think John Aldrich should know it."

"No one, Dr. Drake. Because you wrote the life of Emiliano Zapata, I trust you. That was a work of love. I feel that your beliefs and mine are one. Are they?"

"Yes," I said.

"You love Mexico?"

I nodded. "Almost as much as my own country. In a way it too is my country."

"Then say nothing."

"I won't," I said and stood up.

"The knife," Madero said. "Do you want it?"

"No," I said. I picked it up and let it lie across my palm. "Did you take it apart?"

"Apart?"

"Like this," I twisted the blade and slid it out of the handle. "See. Inside. Cut in the silver is his name."

Then I stopped talking. There was something inside the handle that shouldn't be there. A paper clyinder. He saw it too, took the silver-crusted hilt from me. With the point of his gold pencil he slid the paper out and spread it on the table and both of us stared down at it.

It was old and yellow, that bit of paper, and it had evidently been torn from the page of a manuscript. The writing, almost illegible because the ink was faded, was in archaic Spanish.

"Where the tunnel turns west by north," someone had written—how long ago I could only guess—"there is a large flat stone set high in the wall and above it smaller stones form a crude cross. From that point we followed the tunnel for 152 paces. There at the height of my shoulder was the deep recess we had made. In it we placed the chest, with great effort because of its weight. Then we replaced the stones and filled the crevices with mortar until there was again an unbroken stretch of wall."

An old book, Dorothy Allen had said. Arthur had been

searching for an old, old book. I thought of his letter. "There is something in the wind, something so big I can say nothing about it—if things go well, we'll be rich," he had written. And now this bit of paper, rolled into a cylinder and hidden in the handle of the knife I had made long ago.

Madero was watching me and only his small dark eyes gave indication of the agile mind behind the expressionless face. He touched the paper with his forefinger. "What meaning?"

"I don't know."

"You never saw it before?"

"No."

"And your brother said nothing to you about it?"

"Nothing."

"Tunnels," said Madero. "There are many of them. There is one under the so-called secret convent of Santa Monica in Puebla that leads to the old fort. There is one from the Palace to Chapultepec. I've heard of several in Guadalajara. From one church to another. The clergy liked underground passageways. Why not? The Indians dug them."

Twice someone had gone through my things, I remembered. Last night three men had attacked me in the shadow of the Horse. Was this then what they sought? I said, "This could have nothing to do with my brother's disappearance and the death of Joe Briggs."

"Of course not," Madero said.

"May I take it?"

He glanced at it again and it seemed to me his eyes were photographing it. "Certainly."

I put it in my wallet.

"How long has it been there?" He indicated the hilt.

"I don't know. I made the knife fourteen years ago. Gave it to my brother then. I've never removed the blade since."

"Who knew the trick?"

"I knew it. He did."

Madero fitted the blade into the hilt, couldn't make the two stay together. I took it from him, showed him how it worked.

"Perhaps this was meant for you," Madero observed.

The thought had occurred to me. I tried to keep my expression as blank as his own. "He would have given me some hint."

"And he didn't?"

"No."

"Bit by bit," said Madero with a small smile, "we are adding to the confusion. This is really a peculiar business. A damned peculiar business."

"I'll be getting along," I said.

"You must be careful, Dr. Drake."

"I'll be careful."

"That bit of paper. Someone might want it."

"Nonsense," I said.

"So far, I haven't searched your room," he said pointedly. "But someone else—"

"I'll be careful."

"You are reticent with me," Madero chided. "Be as reticent with others. You can trust them less."

"I'm not reticent with you." I tried to look truthful. His smile was bland and I knew he didn't believe me. I knew that no matter how hard I tried I couldn't wear a mask in his presence. I said good-by and went out into the street, and as the door closed I thought about going back and telling the little man everything I knew. I thought of asking him to go to Arthur's house with me. Then what he had told me about the Sons of Cortez filled me with anger again. No. I would blunder along in my own fashion. I would play it alone. Momentarily I considered showing John Aldrich the bit of old paper. Then Madero's words rang in my ears—"Be as reticent with others." Perhaps he was right. I would go to Aldrich and ask him to help me get Arthur's servants out of the way, but I wouldn't tell him why I wanted the house on the Street of the Crying Woman to myself.

On the way to Aldrich's office I stopped at the Wells Fargo

office and rented a lock box and I put the paper in the box feeling foolish and theatrical. I wouldn't need it anyway. I knew its contents by rote and it occurred to me that so also did José Manuel Madero who by now was probably brooding in the sun with a half-knitted sock in his hands.

TWELVE

THE MIND is a curious thing. It grasps phrases and finds the rhythm in them and then keeps rolling them around and around. Once when I was in college and studying much too hard I almost failed an examination because my mind picked up a jingle that had something to do with punch, punch, punch with care, punch in the presence of the passenger. Walking east on Avenida Madero that day I found myself taking the words the unknown one had written so long ago and giving them a crude rhythm. "Where the tunnel turns west there's a large flat stone, set high in the wall is a large flat stone," the thing went, and I couldn't rid myself of it. It was buzzing about me like a mosquito in the dead of night when I told the wizened old Mexican I would like to confer with Mr. Aldrich.

Aldrich heard my voice and called to me to come in. He was holding the telephone in both hands and his face was redder than usual and his eyebrows fairly bristled.

"Trouble?" I asked.

"The usual," he growled. "Damn Mexico. How are you, boy? Who hit you?"

"Three guys," I said and as I told my story his expression grew grim.

"I don't like it, Mitchell."

"I don't either."

"What were they up to?"

"Someone seems to want something. I can't figure it out."

"You're sure they were after you?"

"Who else?"

"The girl—this what's her name—"

"Penny Gage?" I shook my head. "No reason."

Aldrich grunted. "Dammit, boy. Be more careful. Anything else on your mind?"

"Yes," I said. "I want to get rid of Arthur's servants."

He tugged his ear. "That won't be easy."

"Why?"

He made an angry gesture. "Ever try to fire a servant? Unions. Red tape. Six months' notice. Something like that. That's why I haven't done it. Figured Arthur would turn up. Let's wait a bit."

"No," I said. "I don't like that pair."

"Nor I."

"Get rid of them then. Pay them six months' wages if necessary. I want to close the house."

His eyes probed my face. "Why, Mitchell?"

"I don't like them. That's all."

"All right. If you say so."

"The knife that killed Joe came from that house," I said. "It must have. It just occurred to me."

"You think—" He began biting his mustache.

"That they may know something? Yes."

"Then we shouldn't let them go. We should keep them on tap."

"Let Madero take care of that," I said. "We'll phone him and tell him we're letting them go. He'll keep an eye on them."

He stared moodily at the blotter, nodded finally. "All right. I guess it can be arranged. If you wait a few minutes, I'll take you to lunch. Grab a book and sit tight. I've a couple of things to do."

The cases along the walls were filled with books, but they were law books and didn't seem to have been touched for years. I picked one out at random and sat on the couch with the book open in my lap but I didn't read it. I started in at the beginning and moved forward step by step and mixed up in my thoughts was the beating rhythm of that phrase, like counterpoint—where the tunnel turns west there's a large flat stone.... Excitement swept over me and I wanted to rush out to Arthur's house and start searching. I didn't want lunch. I didn't want to talk to Aldrich. But I checked myself with the thought that I could do nothing until the house was empty. I must wait. Aldrich's voice pushed through the wall of my thoughts.

"It's Miss Allen," he said. "She's been trying to get hold of you." He had the telephone in his hands and covered the mouthpiece with his palm.

"Why?"

"Wants to know if there's anything new. Suppose I ask her to have lunch with us."

"All right," I agreed.

He spoke into the phone, hung up and rose. "I'm ready," he said.

It wasn't far to Prendis. We walked, threading our way through the crowds filling the narrow sidewalks, and Aldrich grumbled about the holes in the walks and the tourists and the government edict which deprived the city of electricity from eleven to two. I listened to him without thinking because my mind was busy with something else. I thought I saw a little light. Not much, but enough to give me hope. Hope of what? Of finding Arthur? Again I was horribly depressed.

Prendis didn't help lift the dark cloud. The restaurant hadn't changed. There in the corner was the table Arthur and I had always taken when we had a little money and could afford the place, though it wasn't expensive. The waiter who had served us flashed a smile in my direction and bobbed his head. He was an old man and he had once worked at the Regis when Father was alive and he had known Father well. Dorothy Allen was waiting for us at a big table against the wall.

"Right after you left last night your friends came in," Dorothy said. "Amaro and Ruiz. I told them you were looking for them."

Aldrich shot a glance at me, raised his eyebrows.

"You been fighting?" Dorothy asked.

"I tripped," I said. We sat down and the old waiter came over and shook hands and asked about Arthur. I told him Arthur was out of town.

Dorothy was watching me, a curious smile playing round her mouth. "Ran into *her* friend, was that it?"

"No," I said.

"Whose friend?" John Aldrich asked, and gave me a puzzled look.

"Miss Allen's just talking," I said.

"She's very pretty," Dorothy said. "I think you're in love with her." I must have blushed, because she giggled and put her hand on mine. "Thanks for asking me to lunch. I was lonely. That's why I called the hotel. I was very lonely."

I glanced at her and thought again how pretty she was. She took her hand away and began tearing off little pieces of French bread and rolling them into balls. Her eyes were very bright. I knew she was thinking about Arthur. I reached across and took the bread away and then caught her hand and held it. When I looked up I saw Penny Gage and her aunt coming toward our table. I released Dorothy's hand and stood up. Aldrich looked around, saw them bearing down on us, and stood up too.

"Hello, Mitchell," Molly Gage said. "Sit down." She was looking at Dorothy appraisingly and the dancer, seeming to sense she was on display, sent a sweet smile toward the older woman.

"Hello, Miss Gage." Dorothy spoke to Penny.

"Good to see you again," Penny said. There was an odd look in her eyes as she flicked a glance at me.

I took care of the introductions. Then they said they were meeting friends and went to a table farther back.

"A jealous wench," Dorothy said.

I told her not to be ridiculous.

"You don't know women," Dorothy said. "They don't want anything until they think someone else wants it."

"Are you that way?"

"I'm practical. I take what I can get. When you've been in show business as long as I have you find it's the only way. You get hard."

"You're not hard."

She laughed. "You don't know me. I'll show you that side sometime. I don't let people push me around."

Aldrich looked up from the menu. "Someone pushing you around?"

"Not yet." She laughed and it seemed to me there was bitterness behind the laughter.

The waiter came back and we gave him our order. Then we talked about Arthur and I tried to make Dorothy remember more about the old book, but it was no use. She said she had told me everything she could remember.

Aldrich peered at me from under his shaggy eyebrows. "You think it might be important now?"

I was on the point of telling them about the paper. I wanted to tell them. Here was Father's attorney, a man I had known for years; here was my brother's financée. If anyone could be trusted, they could. Yet I held back. I remembered Madero's warning and held back. "I don't want to overlook anything," I said. And there we let the matter rest.

Before we went out, I stopped by Penny's table, and said if they were going to be at the hotel later in the day, I'd drop by. I stood there and looked down at Penny and I couldn't seem to find any place to put my hands. Penny didn't speak. She didn't even look at me.

"We'll be there," Molly Gage said. Her smile said she liked me and that helped a little. But not much. I wanted Penny's smile. I wanted Penny to look up at me with her eyes shining. I wanted to see stars mirrored in her eyes again. I said good-by and followed Aldrich and Dorothy out of the place.

A block from the café, Aldrich left us.

"I'll take care of the servant business at once," he said. "They'll be out in a couple of hours."

I thanked him. "Por nada," he said. "Good-by, Miss Allen. If they start shoving you about let me know."

"I can take care of myself," Dorothy said.

I watched him go, his shoulders straight, his cane swinging jauntily, ignoring the beggars and the lottery-ticket sellers, oblivious that this was Mexico and the little people around him owned the land. The old order, I thought. There was a symbol of it. Poor John. The world had changed and he wouldn't change with it. As a youngster he had lived under the rule of Porfirio Diaz and to him that was Mexico—the Diaz era— the good era. A vague suspicion entered my mind. The printing press. Bought with an American Express money order secured here in the capital. I pushed the thought away.

"You're a strange one, Mitchell," Dorothy said. She wasn't looking at me. She was following Aldrich with her glance. "I'm beginning to like you very much."

I thanked her. To cover my confusion I moved to a doorway where the sheets announcing the winners of the last lottery were suspended. I tried to find my numbers but they weren't there. "I've never won anything," I said.

"Nor I. I'm not lucky." Her face was grave and her eyes had bitterness in them.

"Things will turn out all right," I tried to put assurance into my tone, assurance I didn't feel. I was certain things wouldn't turn out all right.

"Why should they?"

"Reward for virtue," I said.

"Oh, sure," Dorothy said. "Some day I'll tell you about my virtue." She plucked at my sleeve and stood there staring up at me, and for a moment I thought she was going to speak. I thought she had something she wanted very much to tell me. She gave a little shrug, wrinkled her nose, and said, "Let's go."

There were some clouds playing tag with the sun and the wind had a bite to it. It came from the east, from the snowfields on the shoulders of Popo and Ixtaccihuatl and the few people who were about hurried along, wrapping their shawls and serapes about their necks, covering their mouths so that the cold air couldn't get to their lungs. Most of the shops had their steel shutters down, for this was siesta time. That gave the city a deserted look.

At the doorway of her apartment house, Dorothy fumbled in her purse and took out an envelope. Amaro's name and address was scrawled on the back of it. "He gave me this last night," Dorothy explained. "He asked if you'd mind stopping by a moment. He said it was important. That's what I called about this morning. I wanted to tell you."

I put the envelope in my pocket. She was standing on the steps of the apartment house and her face was level with my own.

"Good-by," I said.

"Good-by, Mitchell. Be a good boy." Suddenly she put her hands on my shoulders, pulled me toward her and kissed me. "That's for your faith and your sweetness and your blindness," Dorothy said, laughed, and was gone.

A bit bewildered, I stood looking at the closed door. Faith and blindness. More confusion. I shook my head, noted the address on the envelope, and asked myself what Amaro wanted. I was tempted to ignore his request. I kept thinking of the yellowed scrap of paper, and of Arthur's house on the Street of the Crying Woman, and I was impatinet to start my search. But there was no use hurrying. I must wait until the servants were gone. So I caught a cab and gave the driver Amaro's street number.

THIRTEEN

I CLIMBED a short flight of stairs and saw his name on one of the twelve mail boxes in the entrance way and pushed the bell. The annunciator buzzed. I spoke into the tube, told him who

I was. He said to come right up.

He wasn't alone in the small, overly furnished room. Ruiz was there and Jacques Magnin was there and they were drinking aguardiente.

"Drink?" Amaro asked. He looked sullen and unfriendly. I said no and sat down, facing the windows.

"Miss Allen said you wanted to see me."

Amaro threw a glance at Magnin. The writer's eyes were bloodshot and he needed a shave badly. He held his glass in both hands as though to keep them from shaking. Ruiz was slumped in the corner of the soiled, overstuffed couch, smoking a cigarette.

"I did," Magnin said. "Do you want me to die?"

If I had been truthful, I would have said I didn't care much one way or the other. I wasn't truthful. I said, "No, of course not."

"Then for God's sake don't go around looking for me." Magnin spoke passionately, a little desperately. I had thought of him as courageous. He wasn't now. He was frightened, there was no doubt of it. "I don't want to be found. Understand that."

"All right." I started to get up.

"Wait," Magnin said gently. "Sorry, Dr. Drake. I know you were trying to help Miss Gage. I'm upset and there's a reason. I came down here to save my skin." He began pacing the narrow room. "Do you realize what I'm up against?"

"I can guess."

"It's bad." Magnin stopped in front of me and put his finger against his nose as though to push it back in its proper place. "Very bad. They almost got me in the States. So I ran." He waved his left hand. "Oh, I know what you're thinking. I was a fool. I told Miss Gage. But I had to. She is a fine young woman and I didn't want to hurt her. I'm—" He stopped talking.

"You think highly of Miss Gage," I said.

He nodded. "But I think more highly of my life at the moment. I did a very foolish thing, yes. But I expected her to understand. I forgot how young she is and how willful."

"You think they'll trace you through Miss Gage?"

"I know they will."

"Are they here?"

"They may be."

"But you aren't sure?"

"No. I'm not sure. How can I be until someone steps up and lets me have it? I don't know who they are. That's why I'm frightened." He mopped his forehead with his handkerchief. "Believe me, Dr. Drake. I'm not a coward. But I don't like uncertainty. I don't like what I can't fight."

"Has there been an attempt to kill you?"

He shook his head.

Imagination, perhaps, I thought. The man had the jitters. He was letting fear get the upper hand. I asked, "What do you want me to do."

"Ask Miss Gage to go away."

"I'll do that." I would be more than glad to do that. It was one of the few things I could do with genuine relish.

Magnin sighed and there was relief in the sigh. "Would you give her this, please?" He held out an envelope. "I could send it but her aunt might see it. Or someone else might see it."

I put the envelope in my pocket. "I wouldn't worry too much," I said. "Get out of town. Go to one of the little towns off the paved roads. They won't think of looking for you there."

Ruiz spoke. "That was my suggestion."

"It's the thing to do," Magnin agreed. "And please tell Miss Gage this. There's someone following her, I think."

"I don't think," I said. "I know. There's a private detective following her. Her aunt hired him."

"You sure?"

"Yes." Then I knew I wasn't sure. Paul Brent said he was a private detective. I looked up at the man standing in front of me who had fear deep in his eyes. Perhaps he had reason to be terrified. Perhaps the angel-faced Brent was the reason. And then I thought, what of it? It had nothing to do with me. I had my own problems, my own worries and these two men in the room might have some connection with those problems. Who could say? And what did Magnin's life amount to? Certainly he was no admirable character.

"Try and make her understand," Magnin said.

"I'll try." I knew I would. No matter what I thought about him, I knew I would. "But don't stick around. She may decide to stay."

"I have friends," Ruiz said. "I'll send him to them. Anything new about your brother?"

"It was his knife they found in Joe Briggs' back." I watched his expression.

He sat up, looked startled. "Arthur's knife?"

"Yes. The one with the handle made of pesos. Remember it?"

Ruiz nodded. "Do they think he—" He left the rest to my imagination.

"I don't know what they think."

"Impossible," Amaro put in. "Arturo and Briggs. They were friends. Great friends. Arturo wouldn't kill anyone."

"I know it," I said. "But someone wanted to link Arthur with the murder. Someone has been trying to link Arthur with other things."

"So?" Amaro was frowning. "Other things."

"Yes." I didn't explain. I stood up. "I'm beginning to understand a little of it. There is an old book mixed in it somewhere." I looked at the three faces, tried to read what was going on behind those three faces. "An old, old book and an American Express money order," I added. Then I left them and as I walked down the dark stairs I tried to find significance in the glance that had passed between Amaro and Ruiz.

The servants were gone when I reached the Street of the Crying Woman. Aldrich's aged clerk, Ramon de Silva, was standing in the doorway pulling at his wispy mustache and looking doleful.

"Any trouble?" I asked.

"They were paid." He shrugged. "What trouble could there be?"

I thanked him and called a cab and saw him on his way. Then I went inside and bolted the door.

Being alone in the house gave me an odd feeling of uneasiness. It was suddenly horribly empty. And though the others had been gone only a little while, it seemed to have been untenanted for a long time. I went from room to room and the longer I stayed the more I wanted to be out of it. But I remained. There were things to do. Here my brother had been for the last time. Here was the place to start the search for him.

I examined the cupboards, rapped on the walls, pulled at the shelves and slid my hand along the paneling. One by one I inspected the rooms from floor to ceiling, feeling moment by moment more foolish, more like a child playing a foolish game. Secret passageways. Trap doors. Like the convent of Santa Monica where you pulled a shelf away and pushed a button and the whole wall gave. But I didn't stop looking. Arthur had leased the house for a reason and I was certain the reason was the paper cylinder hidden in the haft of the knife.

The house was airless, damp. I opened the door into the patio, went out and stood in the pale sunshine looking at the patch of sky, getting the taste of the place out of my mouth. The patio had been badly neglected. There was a tangle of shrubbery along the walls and the trees were like unkempt old men. In the center was an iron pump, rusty and apparently unused. I went to it and pushed the handle up and down. No water came from the spout, which didn't surprise me. Then I realized that the flagstones around the base of the pump seemed cleaner than the others. I lifted one. There was fresh earth under it. Someone had filled the well in and done it fairly recently.

I was excited now. I circled the patio, looking carefully at the stones and near the rear wall I found what I sought. There the flagstones were large and I began tapping them with a piece of iron. One gave back a hollow sound. I put my fingers under the edge of it and lifted. It came away easily and I stared into a round hole about three feet across. A few feet down was the top of a ladder.

In the top drawer of the dresser in Arthur's room there was a large flashlight. I got it and flashed its beam into the pit. It wasn't deep. Not more than twelve feet and it angled a little toward the west. Here goes, I thought. My feet found the ladder and I climbed down and then I was kneeling on the damp earth, flashing the light into another passageway leading west. Cold air came out to me and I knew I was close to the tunnel. I crawled ahead.

It wasn't far. I had crawled not more than fifteen feet before the passageway ended and I was in another faced with stones. I could stand upright in it and still there was more than a foot above my head.

The light cut a wide path in the darkness. I played it on the walls around me. A big stone with a cross above it, then 152 paces west by north. But where was the stone?

I moved ahead very slowly and perhaps a dozen paces beyond the opening that had been cut into the tunnel. I tripped over a loose stone. I pointed the light pencil down, then dropped on my knees and pulled at the protruding bit of rock. It came away and I could see that it had been taken out not very long ago. The circle of light showed me that others near it had been lifted out too.

I knew then. I didn't need to pull the rocks away and dig into the damp earth. I didn't need to claw down into that evil-smelling ground to know what was lying under it. But I tore at the stones and at the earth. And after a little while I pushed the dirt back and replaced the blocks of granite and sat with my back against the wall. I don't know how long I sat there. I seemed numb, unable to think, unable to feel, wrapped in the damp gloom of the centuries-old tunnel. After a while I put my head on my arms and for the first time in years I cried a little. For I had found my brother—buried a few feet away.

FOURTEEN

IT WAS cold in the tunnel, there under the street where superstitious natives said the ghost of Doña Marina wandered wailing through the darkness, cold and damp and quiet. Off somewhere, water dripped faintly, the drops falling with clocklike rhythm, but there was no other sound. I sat against the wall in the darkness so numbed with grief and horror that time meant nothing, until after a while hot anger kindled itself and spread through my body and I knew what madness was. I got up and plunged toward the opening that led up to Arthur's house, stumbling in the dark with but one thought in mind, murder. Then as I bent down to crawl through the light, sanity returned. I could not kill blindly and unknowing. I had found Arthur's body but I was no nearer the truth than I had ever been. I backed into the tunnel, stood up and switched on the flash light. The paper in the knife. Arthur had hidden it and the man who killed Arthur had killed Joe Briggs not knowing that what he had taken two men's lives for was in his hand. I was certain the murderer still sought the secret of this passageway; but I must make sure.

A stone with a rude cross above it, then 152 paces west by north. Again the light scraped the slimy walls and I moved forward, avoiding the spot where my brother lay, trying to keep my mind clear, examining first one side and then the other. Finally, I found it. On my left, at the height of my shoulder, a square rock three feet across had been fitted into the wall and above it smaller stones made a rough cross pattern. Now there were other ghosts around me, ghosts of the Indians who long ago had labored here, who had fitted these stones together; ghosts of the ones who had come later, straining under a heavy burden and who had counted off 152 paces from this starting place. My legs were long, much longer than those of a man of ordinary stature. I shortened my stride and began counting.

Once anger and grief roared up into my mind and made me lose count; then I returned to the rock and the cross and began again. One hundred—one hundred and thirty—one hundred and fifty. I splashed light on the wall to my right and took two more steps. The wall was no different here than it had been—untouched in centuries. Nowhere within a space of thirty yards had it been disturbed. The secret was still a secret. Behind those stones was that which Arthur had sought, that which he had hoped would give us freedom to wander to the far places of the earth, that which had brought him death. I didn't want it. For all of me it could stay there for eternity. But it had brought Arthur death and now it would bring death to the one who had killed him. Until this place, where unknown men had hidden their treasure, was no longer a secret, the murderer would be close at hand. I unclenched my fists and moved my fingers. Long fingers, long and unnaturally strong. There would be no waiting for the firing squad. I turned and hurried back, stopping only for a moment beside my brother's shallow grave. Then I was in the sunlight again.

Penny was in the lobby of the Reforma hotel sitting in a chair by the elevator with a magazine in her lap. She had on a pale green linen dress and linen shoes with holes in the toes that looked anything but sensible. She wasn't reading. She was watching the door and when I came in she stood up and came to meet me.

She threw words at me. "You saw him? Was he all right? Does he really want me to go away?"

I had to think a moment. I had forgotten Magnin. I had forgotten about the letter I had left in the clerk's care on my way to the house on Santa Maria. "Yes," I said finally.

Her eyes searched my face. "Mitchell. What's the matter, Mitchell?"

"Nothing," I said. "He's all right."

"Your face," Penny said. "So white. And there's dirt on your coat."

"He wants you to go home," I said. "As soon as it's safe, he'll write to you."

"But you?"

"Is your aunt in?"

She nodded. I got into the elevator and she followed me and she was still looking at me. The expression on her face was that of a puzzled child. I tried to speak but the words wouldn't come. There was an ache at the base of my throat that made me inarticulate. We went along the hall, our feet making no sound in the thick carpets and then we were in the sitting room and I found myself sitting on the couch staring at the window and there was a glass of brandy in my hand. Penny and her aunt were standing in front of me, fear in their eyes.

"What is it, Mitchell?" Penny's aunt kept saying. "What is it, son?"

Then she seemed to know, for she sat beside me and put her arm around me and my head was on her shoulder. "Poor, poor boy," Penny's aunt said, and her cool fingers touched my hair. "Poor, dear boy."

I didn't feel so alone now. After a while I sat up and drained my glass and then I could speak calmly.

"Arthur's dead," I said. "I found his body." And I told them about the pit in the yard and the tunnel and the loose stone that had tripped me. Molly Gage sat on one side of me with her arm tight around my shoulders and Penny was on the other and it wasn't for quite a while that I realized she had my right hand tight between her two small ones.

Molly Gage refilled my glass and this time she poured out two more brandies and gave one to Penny. "Who did it, Mitchell?" she asked. She sat in an arm chair in front of me now.

"That's one thing I don't know."

"Start at the beginning," Penny's aunt said. "Tell me everything. Perhaps I can make sense of it."

I told her. Once, when I told about the attack by the Horse, she started to speak, then she waved her hand and I went on. "That's all," I said. "Everything."

She poured out more brandy, stood looking down at me with the decanter in her hand. "Three things are obvious."

I waited. Such a lovely face, I thought, watching her. Kind and wise and beautiful. An older Penny. A wiser Penny. Would the child be like that years hence? Penny was very quiet, so quiet she seemed not to be breathing. I could feel the pulse in her fingers.

"The Dancer—Dorothy—knows," Penny's aunt said. "She knows your brother is dead. I'm sure of that."

"But he wrote her in December from Vera Cruz," I said. "That's one thing I'm certain of."

She moved her hand as though pushing the existence of the letter away. "Two. Joe Briggs was killed because he came to that conclusion about the Allen girl. Only he had proof."

"And the third?"

"I never hired anyone to watch Penny," Molly Gage said.

FIFTEEN

"THERE'S ONE thing to do," Penny's aunt said. She didn't wait for a question. She went to the desk, found the telephone book and riffled through the pages. "What's the first name of this Madero?"

"José Manuel," I said. "And that's the wrong book. He's in the Ericksen directory."

She took out the other. "You call him, Mitchell. All I do is confuse the operators."

Penny took her hands away. I crossed to the phone.

"Tell him to come here," Penny's aunt said. "This is something that should have been done the day you arrived."

I obeyed. I didn't question, because there was a quality in her voice that made me sure it was the right thing to do, the only thing to do. He wasn't home. I told his wife where I was and to try and find him. Then I called the palace and left word. I sat at the desk and looked at the instrument and wondered where the little man was.

"We'll wait," Penny's aunt said. She went into the bedroom and came back with her chess set and put in on the coffee table by the couch. I helped her place the men, hid a pawn in each hand. She pointed to my right. I opened my hand. "I defend," I said.

She moved a pawn to king's four. I brought my king's knight out.

"Alekhine's defense," she said. "Every time you use it, you win." She drew one eyebrow down. "Do you realize that everything you've done in this case has been right, Mitchell? Like this defense. You've allowed yourself to be pushed around the board and now a weakness has developed. A very vital weakness."

"It was unconscious," I said. "Besides, everything I've done hasn't been right. I've been blundering around tripping over things." Pain stabbed at me and I shut my eyes.

"Your move," Penny's aunt said.

I had moved fourteen times when the phone rang. Penny got up and answered it. "Send him right up," she said.

Molly Gage took my queen. "Check."

I studied the board. I was still studying it when Madero's knuckles tapped on the door. We stood up and Molly Gage told him to come in.

He bobbed his head at us, closed the door behind him, crossed to the table and looked down at the board. "Black should take the queen with the king," he said. "Not with the rook. Right?"

"Right," Molly Gage said.

I introduced them and he bowed and smiled. "I am very pleased," Madero said.

"Sit down, Mr. Madero," Molly Gage said. "Brandy?"

"Thank you." He sipped the brandy, shook his head. "Soon no more of this, eh? Soon only Mexican brandy. One of the crosses we must bear when a democracy falls. You wished to see me?"

Molly Gage nodded. "Tell him, Mitchell."

Again I told my story. There was much he knew already. There was much he didn't know. He sat hunched over, nursing his glass, staring at the black and white men on the chess board as though the unfinished game was of much more importance than what I had to say. I finished. My throat was dry and in me there was the knawing ache put there by grief. In Molly Gage's eyes there was tenderness and compassion. I looked at Penny and saw tears.

"I should call you foolish," Madero spoke gently. "But no. I understand, Dr. Drake. I would have held back too, I think. No matter. There is time. There is time as long as the wall is untouched, as long as the stones keep their secret. Have you the letter to the girl?"

I took it from my wallet. He glanced at it, nodded, gave it back. "The girl gave you this?"

"She gave it to John Aldrich."

"You're sure your brother wrote it?"

"Quite sure."

"How long have Aldrich and the Allen girl known each other?"

"She came to him with the letter a short time ago. He wrote me at once to come to Mexico. Or so he says."

"How about Ruiz? And Amaro? How well does Miss Allen know them?"

"That I can't say. They often go to the El Toro."

He kept hammering at me with questions. He wanted everything. Questions that dug into the far past and the immediate past and the present. Questions about Magnin, and Paul Brent. He shot them at me steadily and all the time he kept his eyes on the unfinished chess game and his interest in the little men seemed so great that I wondered if he heard my answers. The questions stopped. The room was silent.

"It is clearer," he said then. "But not clear enough. Still confusion." He emptied his glass. "That is lovely brandy."

Molly Gage refilled the glass. She put a trace of a smile on her lips. "Is it true you knit?"

He nodded vigorously. "Why not? One needn't think when one is knitting. Think about what one is doing with one's hands, I mean." He touched the chess board. "This. It takes the whole mind. I knit and read mystery novels and play checkers with my daughters and then I can think. My grandfather. I learned the trick from him."

"You know the murderer?" Penny spoke for the first time.

He regarded her gravely. "Two things bother me. There should have been no fighting by the Horse. I can't connect that with the murder. And who searched Dr. Drake's room in Woodland." He made an airy gesture. "No point. Unless—"

"Unless what?" Penny asked a little breathlessly. It seemed to me she was afraid of the answer.

He shrugged. "Never mind."

I was puzzling over the whole business when the telephone rang. Molly Gage answered it. "For you." She spoke to Madero.

Carefully he put his glass on the table. Then he picked it up quickly and wiped the bottom of it with his handkerchief, throwing a knowing look in my direction, rose and went to the phone. "Bueno," he said.

Three pairs of eyes watched him. His frown deepened. He shoved his right hand into his pocket, took out his cigarette case and with that quick gesture which always startled me flipped a cigarette into his mouth. He didn't light it. Then he put the receiver back.

"A shooting," he said. "Another thing to worry me. Your friend Mr. Magnin has been shot."

Penny moaned. She sat down and put her head in her hands. "I've killed him," she cried. "Oh, I've killed him."

SIXTEEN

EVEN IF she had led to Mexico the men who wanted Magnin out of the way, Penny hadn't killed him. He wasn't dead, though it was only because of the deity that watches over rogues, drunkards and fools that he had escaped. Two bullets had plowed through his body and the breeze from both of them must have fanned his heart as they went by.

"Right through the chest," said Madero as he turned from the phone. "The doctor is quite excited about it. He is a pistol enthusiast. Says he never saw such beautiful marksmanship."

"Stop," Penny said. "Please stop."

"I beg your pardon," Madero said. "I must go. Perhaps you would like to go with me?" I knew from his tone he wanted me to go.

"Yes," I said. I patted Penny's shoulder and we went out into the hall. "Who?" I asked.

He shrugged. "No one seems to know." He cocked his head on one side. "Perhaps you can offer a suggestion."

"Perhaps," I said. But I offered none.

There was a crowd in front of Amaro's apartment house but no one was particularly excited. After all, it was only a shooting, nothing to get upset over. Only one man had been shot and he wasn't dead. They shrugged their shoulders, smoked cigarettes and got in the way. Near by, an old woman had brought up her charcoal brazier and griddle and was cooking tacos.

We pushed our way through the good-natured throng to the steps where two police sat looking down at a little pool of blood. They got up and touched their caps respectfully.

"Who saw it?" Madero asked.

One of the policemen jerked his thumb toward the door. "A gentleman who calls himself Amaro. He is with my superior. And that one." He pointed to a scrawny boy with greasy black hair and a smudge on his nose squatting on his shine kit. The boy leaped up.

"I saw it. Right there I was standing." He pointed a few yards west. "They sang by me like bees, the bullets. I would have given not a tostón for my life at the moment."

"Tell me," Madero said. He squatted on his heels, gave the boy a cigarette and lit one for himself.

"Shine?" said the boy.

"Thank you, no. Not at the moment."

"The shoes are soiled," said the boy.

"No," Madero said.

"I was there," the boy said. "In the sun, sitting. Two gentlemen came through the door and stood at the top of the steps. Bang, bang. One gentleman rolled down the stairs like a beer barrel."

"And you?"

"I was lying in the sunlight," the boy said.

"Did you see the assassin?"

"A glimpse. A man it was. He—" The boy snapped his fingers. "Gone like that."

"You're a great help," Madero said. "The government should honor you."

"It was nothing. Like bees they were, those bullets."

"Where was the man standing? He with the gun?"

"Yonder." The boy pointed across the street and east. "In the shadow of the doorway."

"The bullets then went in circles to buzz past your ears?"

The boy grinned. "The gentleman does not believe?"

"He believes," Madero said.

"I was wearing the medal," the boy said. "The medal bearing the image of the patron saint of shine boys." His grin grew broader.

"Go on with you," Madero said. He rose and I followed him upstairs.

Ruiz was gone. Amaro and an officer were in the apartment and when he saw me Amaro glowered and muttered something under his breath. His eyes said I was to blame. I didn't disillusion him. The officer saluted Madero.

"Good afternoon," the officer said.

"I am José Manuel Madero," Madero told Amaro.

"Yes." You could tell Amaro knew that already.

"Your friend. Why was he shot?"

Amaro shrugged. "I know not."

"You saw the man?"

"A glimpse. He was far away. Across the street and east."

"A beautiful shot," the officer said. "A remarkable shot. Sixty yards at least. With a pistol. Ho. Right by the heart. You could put a peso over the holes."

"Would you know the man should you see him again?" asked Madero.

"No," Amaro said. "We were talking, Magnin and I. Two shots. He rolled down the stairs. I saw a man running."

"Which way?"

"East."

"A young man?"

"How can one know?"

Madero's gesture was the habitual one of the Indian. How could one know, indeed? How could one know anything?

"What now?" the officer asked.

"We have taken enough of Mr. Amaro's time. We will leave him." Madero bowed. "Thank you."

"For nothing," Amaro said.

In the hall, Madero screwed up his face. "This does not belong either," he said. "More to confuse me when I should not be confused." He spoke to the officer. "Watch him."

"Of course," the officer said. We went downstairs and now the crowd had thinned. The old woman was still there cooking tacos and the shine boy was there and there was a man with a little coffin on his shoulder. I thought of Paul Brent's aversion to coffins and bull fights, and for the first time in hours, I smiled.

"I shall talk to Mr. Magnin," Madero said. "That will take some time, I'm afraid. An hour. Two. Then a few odds and

109

ends. Your brother's servants. I shall talk to them, too."

"I don't think they killed my brother," I said.

"Nor I. Come on. I'll drop you at the hotel."

"Thanks," I said.

"And if you see Miss Allen, don't mention finding your brother's body."

"I won't."

I was desperately tired. I wanted to feel hot water spurting over me and to stretch out on the bed and sleep, though I knew I wouldn't sleep. I felt as thought I would never sleep again. I got my key and stood in the elevator with my eyes shut. Now the excitement of the Magnin shooting was over, I felt drained of all capacity to feel and think. I fitted the key in the lock, opened the door and stepped into the dark room. My fingers found the light switch and flicked it on. Then I pushed myself back against the door.

Stretched out on my bed was the man with the angel face and there was a revolver in his hand. He was smiling.

"Hello, Mitchell," he said. "You have company."

SEVENTEEN

"YOU WERE out and the bathroom window was open," he said, sitting up and stretching. "How do you stand these inside rooms?"

"They're cheap," I said. "The police are looking for you."

"That's sweet of them."

"They'll find you."

"They'll watch the railroad stations and the roads and the airports," Paul said. "They won't think of looking in your room."

I sat on the corner of the bed. The gun was within easy reach and he had his hands locked behind his head.

"I did you a favor, Mister. You should thank me."

"Your shots were a little to the right," I said. "He isn't dead. And I don't think he's going to die."

He said, "Damn."

"You might as well tell me who you really are," I said.

"Paul Brent," he said.

"With the Argosy Detective Agency," I said.

"Nope. I had the cards printed just in case. A man who follows people around needs an excuse now and then."

"How do you fit into my brother's death?" The gun was lying butt toward me. I had only to reach out and take it.

"Death?"

"I found his body today."

A shadow crossed his face. His eyes grew somber. "I'm sorry, Mister."

"Where do you come in?"

"I don't."

He expected me to believe him. Could I? I stared into his eyes. I said, "Yes, I know. That's why I haven't picked up your gun."

He laughed hollowly, without humor. "I like you, Mister. I don't like many people. That's one reason I'm here. I dropped in to say good-by. I dropped in to see if there were any little jobs I could do before I beat it."

"Three items puzzle Madero," I said. "My room was searched in Woodland. He doesn't understand that. He doesn't understand what happened by the Horse. And he doesn't understand the Magnin shooting. He said these things confuse him. He says they don't fit."

"I searched your room," Paul said. "I got wind you knew Magnin. He had departed from Woodland so I had a look at your belongings. Wanted to see if he had written to you. The only letter I could find was your brother's. Sorry about that."

"It's all right."

"And I'm sorry about your head. I hired those three guys to muss you up a little. So I could step in and rescue you. Gain confidence. It worked. You know about the Magnin shooting."

"Not everything," I said. "Did they hire you to do it?"

He spoke matter-of-factly. My accusation didn't anger him. "I don't kill for dough. You should be able to figure that out. When I kill, it's for a reason."

"And?"

"It goes back a ways." Paul found bitterness, spread it on his words. "Quite a ways. You've read his book?"

"Yes."

"Remember his story about the longshoreman's strike in New York? Six guys were killed in that mess. Another got his back broken. Four went to the can. I was one of the guys who went to the can. I'll take a smoke now." I gave him one, held the match for him. "Thanks. Five years, Mister. And the guy whose back was broken was my old man. Did you ever see a man with a broken back? He isn't dead but he'd be much better off dead. My old lady takes care of him. My old lady and the neighbors. When I was in jail she had to work so they could eat."

I didn't say anything. I sprawled across the foot of the bed and watched him through the smoke. He didn't look angelic now. He looked tired and bitter.

"We weren't reds," Paul said. "Not one of us. They were pushing us around on the docks and a guy named Joe Stein came along and pretty soon he had us raising hell. My old man tried to stop him. He had it figured out. Had Stein pegged for what he was." He shrugged. "It happened. When I got out I started looking for Stein. So did a lot of others. Then Magnin wrote a book and we knew he was Stein." He was silent for a moment, his head pressed against the wall, his eyes on the ceiling. "We talked it over," he went on. "The boys who had done time and the relatives of the dead ones and the boys who went through it all. I said I'd knock him off." He took the gun and balanced it on his palm. "We traced him to Woodland. We found out he had followed that girl to Woodland. Then we lost him. You know the rest."

"Who told you Magnin came to Mexico?"

"No one," Paul explained. "The Gage girl rented a box at the Woodland post office. I got into the box one night and there was a letter from Magnin from Mexico City. So down I came. But I couldn't find him. Then you showed and she showed and it was a cinch. You told me who his friends were. This afternoon I hung around Amaro's apartment and pretty soon out they came and I let him have it. You sure he'll live?"

"The doctor said so."

"It must have been the angle," Paul said. "I shouldn't have missed at that distance."

"And now?"

"I've a job to finish, Mister."

"You haven't a chance," I said. "Madero is on your trail. I told Madero about you and what you looked like. I didn't know."

"I should have explained," Paul said. "Don't fret about it. You've got enough to worry over. Where did you find your brother?"

"In a tunnel under his house," I said.

"The one on Santa Maria?" He saw amazement in my glance. "I followed you out there. I told you I thought you and Magnin were buddies."

"That's the house," I said.

"Tunnel?"

"An old one. Runs from a monastery to a church."

"Let's have it all," Paul said.

I sat up and stretched my legs. It was hot in the room, hot and airless. I thought of Molly Gage's remark about the Alekhine defense. It wasn't true, really. Blundering rather. Jumping around with no purpose. But so far it had worked. So I told him. About the old book and the bit of paper in the handle of the knife. I didn't tell him the directions on that paper. But I told him about the treasure and about the pit in the garden and the protruding stone in the tunnel floor.

"So it's still there," Paul said.

"Yes."

"And he'll go looking for it again?"

"I think so."

"So do I," Paul said. "The thing to do is wait. Wait and watch. It's a cinch, Mister."

"I know how you felt about Magnin," I said. "You wanted to do it yourself. That's the way I feel."

"Don't mess it up, though," Paul said. "Don't do what I did."

"I won't." I looked at my watch, saw that it was past six, picked up the phone. I gave the operator Dorothy's number and then her voice came over the wire. I said, "This it Mitchell Drake."

"Hello, Mitch darling."

"I'm coming by at seven," I said. "I've something to tell you."

"What? About Arthur?" Her voice was faint.

"Indirectly," I said. "I think I have a piece of that book." I could hear her excited gasp. "Wait there for me," I said and hung up.

Paul was standing by the bed, stretching. "I'm going."

"Where?"

"I have a place to hide. A fine place." He smiled.

"Leave town," I said. "Have you any money?"

"Plenty. Have you?"

"Sure," I said.

"Don't be a sucker," Paul said. "About the girl. Gage."

"I won't. And don't try to get Magnin. You haven't a chance."

He shrugged. "Maybe not. But I can try."

"You'll have a time getting out of Mexico."

"There are boats when I need them," Paul said. "You forget I was a longshoreman. Vera Cruz isn't far." He put his gun in his pocket, held out his hand. "Luck, Mister." There was affection in his voice. I felt close to him. I felt I had found a friend.

"Thanks, Paul."

"Don't let things get you down."
"I won't."
He squeezed my hand and was gone.

EIGHTEEN

DOROTHY ALLEN had company. I knew from the tone of her voice when I announced myself through the tube in the entrance hall. She pushed the buzzer that opened the front door and I went upstairs and she was waiting for me in the doorway of her apartment. She put her fingers to her lips. I looked past her and saw Madero sitting on the couch.

"Days go by and I see no one," Dorothy said brightly. She held on to my arm. "Then two gentlemen call at almost the same time." She closed the door.

It was an old place with high windows looking out on the street and there was only one room. A curtain in the corner was awry and you could see a gas plate and some pots and pans. On a stand between the two windows was Arthur's picture and there was a tiny vase with one flower in it in front of the picture.

"I'll only be a moment," Madero said. "Do you mind, Dr. Drake? I've a few questions to ask." He sat very stiffly and his feet just touched the floor. Dorothy put herself on the arm of the battered Morris chair in which I sat. I felt the pressure of her fingers on my shoulder.

"Go ahead," I said.

"There has been a shooting," Madero said. "A very peculiar shooting indeed. You know Mr. Amaro, Miss Allen?"

She was frowning at the little man. Her fingers dug into my shoulder. "Slightly."

"Today Mr. Amaro was with a Mr. Magnin. When Mr. Amaro and Mr. Magnin left the apartment house, someone shot Mr. Magnin. You know him too?"

"I've met him."

"Perhaps you can help me."

"No." Her voice was very low.

"They were patrons of the El Toro?"

"I saw them there on one or two occasions."

"And Mr. Ruiz? You saw him there too?"

She nodded. I knew she was looking down at me. I stared at my hands.

"Often?" said Madero.

"Quite often. I think Mr. Ruiz has an interest in the El Toro."

"So?" He hesitated as though wondering what to say next. He added: "You were a friend of Dr. Drake's brother?"

"He—" there seemed to be fear in her voice—"You've found him?"

"No, Miss Allen. We have not found him."

"You think he—he is mixed up in this shooting?"

"There was a murder," Madero's voice was as expressionless as his face. "Today there was a shooting. Dr. Drake's brother chooses to evade us. What is one to think, Miss Allen?"

She cried out, "No, he didn't."

"Perhaps not. When did you see him last?"

"Late in October."

"Not since?"

"No."

"Has he communicated with you?"

Her fingers signaled to me. I said, "Tell him, Dorothy."

"Yes," Dorothy said. "In December. He wrote to me in December."

"The letter," Madero said. "You have it?"

"I have it," I said and I wondered what he was up to. I took it from my wallet, crossed the room and gave it to him, then returned to the chair. Dorothy's hand sought my shoulder again.

"This was written last year?"

"In December of last year."

"It says December 28 but not the year," Madero said.

"I received it January 1 of this year."

He studied the letter. "Vera Cruz. He wrote it from there?"

"Yes."

"What was he doing in Vera Cruz?"

"I don't know."

"For all you know, he may still be there?"

"I don't know where he is." She was close to tears now and her voice was barely audible.

"Strange," said Madero. "Very strange."

"Find him," Dorothy cried out. "Please find him."

"We are trying, Miss Allen."

"I want to help you. I know he has done nothing wrong. Mitchell told me you were looking for him but I know he has done nothing wrong."

"We shall see." Madero stood up. "Thank you, Miss Allen. I shall keep this letter for a day or so. Yes?"

She slumped back. "Yes."

"I shall return it. Good evening." He bobbed his head, threw a smile at us and was gone. We heard his light steps on the stairs, sat in silence until they faded out.

"Oh, Mitchell," Dorothy said and put her face against my shoulder. "What does it mean?"

"I don't know."

"Poor darling."

"Don't cry," I said. "Please don't cry. We'll find him."

"I know we won't," Dorothy said. "I know he's dead."

"Don't," I said.

She sat up. "Thank God you're here." I saw grief in her face, and wondered. I saw tears on her cheeks and thought Madero might be wrong, Molly Gage might be wrong. And there came into my mind the feeling that the plan I had evolved was a betrayal. Arthur had loved this girl, had planned to marry her. But he was dead. His body lay in the cold darkness and the one who had murdered him was close by waiting to strike again. I thought of Joe and knew I must go through with it. I said, "Dorothy, I found something very strange today. I don't know what to make of it."

She didn't speak. She looked at me, put her hand up and brushed the tears away.

I said, "Hidden in the box with Arthur's shirt studs there was a key. A key to a lock box at the Wells Fargo office. I had the box opened today. There was a piece of paper in the box. That was all."

She got off the arm of the chair and stood in front of me. She was staring at me, her lips parted a little. A lock of her bright hair fell across her forehead.

I took from my pocket the yellowed bit of paper I had retrieved from the box in the Wells Fargo office half an hour before and put it in her hand. She read it, frowning. She read it two or three times then her gaze questioned me.

"I don't know," I said. "It means something important. You mentioned an old book. I think this is the key. I think this is the part of a page from that old book." I took the paper from her.

"Let me read it again," Dorothy said. She studied it, then handed it back and I returned it to my wallet.

"Something is hidden somewhere," I said. "Without the book, there's no way of knowing. And without this bit of paper the book would be valueless. "We've got to find the book, Dorothy."

"But where?"

"If Arthur is alive, he has it. If he isn't, the one who killed Joe Briggs has it."

"Yes," she said softly. She put her face in her hands and there was silence in the room. In the street, a child laughed shrilly.

"Does he know? Madero. About the paper?"

"No," I said.

"Should we tell him?"

"I don't know."

118

"He's very clever, isn't he?"

"I think so."

"Perhaps we should wait a little," Dorothy said. "Do you think we should wait, Mitchell?"

"I guess so."

"If he's dead, who could have killed him?"

"Someone who knew him well."

"Oh no." Her voice was plaintive. "No, Mitchell. He had done nothing. Why? Why?"

"Money," I said. "That's usually the reason for murder. Money or hatred or jealousy. But who would have hated him or been jealous of him."

Her head rested against my arm and a sob shook her body. I put my arm around her, felt the warmth of her and knew the good scent of her hair.

"I still have you," Dorothy said. "Don't go away, darling. You'll help me, won't you? You'll always help me."

"Yes," I said.

"You're so dear," Dorothy said. "So very dear."

I kissed her hair and then I stood up. In the apartment across the street they had turned the radio on and I could see a couple dancing. I wanted to yell at them, to tell them to stop. I didn't. I said, "Good night, Dorothy."

"Please stay," she said. She stood up and held both my arms.

"I can't. I promised to have dinner with Miss Gage and her aunt."

"You love her. Don't you love her?"

"Yes," I said.

"I'm glad." Her eyes had darkness in them. "Don't let her go away, Mitchell. If you love someone, don't lose them."

Pain swept through me. Betrayal, I thought. This grief of hers wasn't feigned. She loved Arthur. Even the blind could see that.

"I've found out what love is," Dorothy said.

"I know."

119

"No," Dorothy said and put an odd smile around her lips. "No, Mitchell. But you will. Kiss me."

I bent down. Her lips were warm and soft. Her arms were tight around my neck. Then she pushed me away.

"Now go," she said in a strangled voice. "Quickly, Mitchell." And she pushed me toward the door.

I stood outside for a moment. "You don't know," she had said. "But you will." What had she meant? I wanted to go back and ask her. But I didn't. I sighed and went downstairs.

I tried to think clearly. I tried to convince myself that in setting this trap I was in no way unfaithful to the memory of my brother. If she was guiltless, there would be no trap. If not? A voice intruded. A voice I knew.

I was passing the tobacco shop a block from Dorothy's apartment. Leaning against the counter, playing dominoes with the shriveled old woman in charge of the place, was Madero, and an unlighted cigarette hung from his lower lip.

"I waited," Madero said. "I thought you might be lonely."

NINETEEN

WE WALKED north on Bolivar. It was raining a little and the few people on the streets hurried along and covered their faces. He nodded toward a man with his serape hiding his mouth. "I feel the urge to pull my serape close around me too," Madero said. "Superstition. Witch doctors. No amount of knowledge changes the Indian. Why did you call on Miss Allen?"

"She wanted to see me."

"Why?"

"She was lonely."

"At this point, one should do nothing rash," Madero said.

"No," I said.

"Civilization, Dr. Drake," Madero said. "I no longer wear

a serape. I no longer cover my face against the damp. There is the law."

"I don't understand."

"One allows the law to mete out punishment."

"Of course," I said.

"It is the safer way," Madero said. "The civilized way. You are an American."

"I was born in Mexico. In a sense I'm a Mexican."

"Only in a sense. What plan have you made?"

"None."

He laughed, mirthlessly.

"The case is in your hands," I said. "I've blundered enough."

"Good," Madero said. From his pocket he took the knife I had made long ago. "This you should keep."

"Thanks." I put it in my belt. The blade was cold against my thigh.

"Some chess at my club? Eh?"

"No," I said. "Not tonight. I have to see someone. I'll be at the Reforma."

He stopped under a street lamp and smiled up at me. "The older one is very wise."

"Yes."

"The young one is foolish now. But not for long."

"Good-by," I said. "I'll see you tomorrow."

He raised his hand and turned away. I watched him hurrying along the wet street and it seemed to me he was bending his head and pulling his jacket up to cover his mouth. I may have been mistaken. A cab drew alongside.

"Mister," the driver said softly. "A hot joint, Mister I take you to a real hot joint."

I got in. "The Reforma," I said.

"But Mister," he protested. "A fine hot joint I know."

"I am no tourist," I said in Mexican.

"Pardon me, señor," he replied.

Penny and her aunt were not in their rooms. I thought

about Magnin and wondered if Penny had gone to see him, and darkness closed down on me. I went into the lobby, but they weren't there. Then I went to the Maya Room and some of the gloom vanished because they were at a table near the windows.

The room was crowded and most of the diners were Americans. The orchestra was playing something I didn't recognize. It was loud, but it was better than *South of the Border*. Despite the decor, the room wasn't Mexican. It didn't even smell Mexican. I glanced through the windows and saw the lights of the city and wondered why tourists hated to be reminded they were in another country.

Penny didn't look up when I reached the table. Molly Gage took my hand and patted it and told me to sit down.

"I can only stay a moment," I said.

Then Penny's eyes were on my face. "Where are you going?"

"Out," I said.

"With Madero?" Molly Gage asked.

"Alone," I said.

"Don't be a fool," Molly Gage snapped.

"I won't."

"Have they"—Penny's eyes had a strange light in them—"arrested anyone?"

I shook my head. "Not yet."

"Who called me, Mitchell?"

"Called you?" I asked. "When?"

"A little after six," Penny said. "A man."

"What did he want?"

"To talk," Penny said. "Is it true?"

"What?"

"Someone called about Magnin," Molly Gage interrupted. "Tell him, Penny."

The girl's voice was faint. "He said awful things. He said Jacques was a —a rat."

"Well," said Molly Gage. The word was expressive.

I knew who had called her and the knowledge gave me

122

warmth. I thought of him sitting on my bed, smiling. A strange man, Paul Brent. Shooting a man down coldly. Shuddering at the sight of a coffin. Then pausing in his flight to do one he scarcely knew a favor. I said, "That was the man who tried to kill Jacques Magnin."

"Then he wasn't telling the truth?"

"You've read the book," Molly Gage said angrily. "Are you blind, Penny? Of course he was telling the truth."

"The man with the angel face called you," I said. "He was in my room waiting for me this afternoon. He told me his reason for wanting to kill Magnin."

"He could be lying," Penny said.

"He could be." The waiter was at my elbow. I ordered brandy and coffee.

"He wasn't," Molly Gage announced. "Did Magnin kill your brother, Mitchell?"

"No."

"Who did?"

"I don't know."

"The girl's mixed up in it? Isn't she?"

"I don't know that. Madero thinks so. I'm sure he does. I've just come from her place and I don't know what to think."

"She cried," Molly Gage said. "Didn't she cry?"

"Yes. She loved Arthur."

Anger flickered in Penny's eyes. "You believe her," she said. "Because she's pretty you believe her."

"You have to believe someone," I said.

Molly Gage looked at me and then she looked at Penny. She said, "I hope you didn't talk too much tonight."

"I didn't. I set a trap," I said.

Penny put a little frown between her eyes. She said, "Don't —" then stopped.

"It has nothing to do with him," I said.

"I didn't mean that."

"Good night," I said, and left them.

TWENTY

A BLOCK away from the house I got out and paid the driver. Then I walked along the dark street, keeping close to the wall. The Street of the Crying Woman was deserted. I stopped in a doorway and looked all around. But there was no one following. Then I went quietly to the door, unlocked it and slipped inside.

I began to know what fear was. The house seemed to reek of death and as I moved forward I felt the terror of the unknown, the same terror a child has when he runs along a road and hears the clatter of his feet on the stones and mistakes it for the footsteps of another. I patted my hip and tried to find comfort in the feel of the knife, but it made me think of Joe and how Joe had died. It made me think of Arthur. Perhaps Arthur's blood was on the blade too. I wanted to throw it from me. I moved out into the patio and now there was a rent in the clouds and moonlight filtered through to put a ghostly pallor on the matted vines and the uneven flagstones. I found the flash where I had left it on a bench by the kitchen door and put it in my jacket pocket, crossed the garden and lifted the stone that covered the pit.

A week before I would not have put my foot on the ladder, I would not have forced myself down into that well of darkness. Fear would have driven me back into the world of light and people. But now terror was not enough to stop me. What had happened was a wind fanning the flames of my anger and hatred. Again I patted the knife and now the feel of it was good. Obsidian as sharp as steel. This time, no sacrifice. Justice instead. Slowly I climbed down and when I was below the level of the earth I pulled the flagstone over the entrance, blotting out the patch of sky, wrapping myself in awful darkness.

I felt my way down, found earth with my feet. Cold air pushed me as I crawled ahead. Then my hands touched stones, damp with the slime of centuries, and I was near the spot where Arthur lay. I knelt there for a moment. Lonely here. So very lonely. No flowers for him. No prayers. I went into the past and found a little one we used to say and my mind told it to him. Then I stood up and moved along the tunnel, touching the wall to my left, searching for the big stone with the cross above it.

Even in the dark it wasn't hard to find. Then I started walking, counting my paces and all around me there were little sounds, like ghostly footsteps. I told myself it was water dripping down. I kept telling myself it was water falling from the ceiling. And the mind knew that was true but the heart didn't.

One hundred. What was that behind me? I stopped and pressed myself against the wall. Only the whisper of the water as it crept through the crevices above me. Or a rat racing away. One hundred and ten—one hundred and twenty. Again the faint scuffling on the stones. No, nothing. My chest hurt from the beating of my heart and the fingers of terror closed my throat so I could hardly breathe. One hundred and fifty. This was it. The trap and me the bait. My hand found the hilt of the knife.

But I didn't draw it. Steel dug into my chest and light blinded me. I blinked and looked down. A hand with a gun in it was there and it was the nose of the gun that was cold against my body.

Fool, I thought. I shouldn't have stopped at the Reforma. I should have come here at once. But I knew why I had stopped. I knew that I had expected something like this, that I wanted to see her once more.

I wasn't afraid now. This was reality. No ghosts. No shadows following. The gun was steel and under the glove that hand that held the gun was flesh and there was an arm and a body and the body belonged to the man who had murdered my brother and my friend. I swung both arms and hurled him back and the gun stabbed at me with a blade of flame.

The shot roared around me, went echoing down the tunnel. I felt blood warm on my shoulder. Then I knew that bravery would net me nothing, so I ran.

Light pursued me, tried to find me. I rounded the bend, started dodging back and forth across the tunnel and the light was after me. I glanced back. Then something hit my shins and I went down. The blast of a shot was right above me. I rolled away and the tunnel swelled with the sound of shots. Then the light went out.

I lay against the wall, waiting for death. The echoes faded. Someone groaned once. Someone was close to me, lying on the stones. I reached toward the sound and my hand touched hair, slid down across a forehead.

"Hello, Mister," a voice whispered. "Leave it there, Mister. Your hand. It's cool, your hand."

I said, "Paul."

"Yes, Mister."

"You, then?"

"No. Not me."

I moved close to him. "Don't take your hand away," Paul said.

"Did he get you, Mister?" Paul asked. His voice was the husk of a voice.

"I'm all right."

"I can taste death," Paul said. "I think I know why."

"Quiet," I whispered.

"He's gone," Paul replied. Then he was silent for a while. I could feel the pulse in his forehead. I pushed his hair back. Somewhere there was water dripping steadily.

"I was in the garden," he said after a while.

"Why, Paul?"

"Hiding out." There were gaps between the words as though he had to grope for them. "I told you I had a safe place to hide. You gave me the idea, Mister. There was a pit if people came. I had a job to finish so I came out here to wait until I could finish it. Then you showed up."

"So you followed me," I said. "Why, Paul?"

"To help the birds cover you with leaves if you got lost," he said, and tried to laugh. "You're a babe in the woods, Mister. I figured you might need help."

"Don't talk, Paul," I said.

"Who was he?"

"I don't know."

"I hurt like hell. And I can taste death. Did you ever taste death?"

"No," I said. "Where's your gun? He may come back."

"Here by my right leg."

I groped for it, found it. There was a hot iron digging in my left shoulder.

"I'm going to die, Mister," Paul said.

"No."

"My old woman may need help. The address is in my pocket."

"Don't worry about her."

"I won't now."

"I'll go get help," I said.

"No. Don't go. I hate darkness."

"You need a doctor. I won't be long."

"It's no use," Paul said. "Please stay."

"All right," I said. I moved close to him and lifted his head and held it in my lap. Then I touched my fingers to his lips. There was someone moving close at hand. I bent and put my lips against his ear and whispered, "Quiet." There was no need. He was dead.

TWENTY-ONE

MY LEFT arm was stiff and when I put the flashlight into my left hand the pain was so bad I had to bite my lips to keep from yelling. Someone was moving behind me and to the right. I turned and pointed the revolver toward the sound and waited. I thought of the pit and knew someone had climbed into the pit and was crawling into the tunnel. Then I flicked on the light. Madero's head protruded from the hole in the tunnel wall.

"I'm here," I said. Light stabbed at me.

"You live then?" Madero's monotone echoed around me.

"Yes."

The light swept over Paul's body. "And this one?"

"No."

"Ah. He of the angel face."

"He was waiting to finish his job," I said. "Hiding in my brother's house. He saw me and followed."

"Fool." Madero found emotion. He hurled the word at me.

I realized then what was in his mind. "I didn't kill him," I said. But in my heart I knew I had. It was my fault he was dead. Another blunder. A trap that had caught not the murderer but the man lying close to me.

"I set a trap," I said. "I came down here to find the man who killed my brother. He was waiting for me in the dark. He shot me and I ran. He shot again and Paul Brent got between me and the bullet."

Madero flashed his light on my shoulder. "A bad one?"

"No."

He pulled my coat aside and ripped the shirt. Then he took the handkerchief from his breast pocket and made a pad of it and tied it over the wound with strips of the shirt. "The other one. Did he get away?"

"I think so."

"I'll have a look." He started walking away and suddenly my mind was clear. I called out, "Wait, come back."

He turned and pointed the light at me.

"I set a trap," I said. "I used Dorothy Allen to bait it for me."

He understood. He caught my right hand and helped me to my feet, then scurried to the hole in the wall and plunged into it. I followed and the pain sent a wave of nausea through me. At the top he waited and pulled me up and I saw the sky again. The clouds were gone and the round disk of the moon was like a silver concha on a pale blue saddle blanket.

"Your shoulder?" Madero asked.

"It's all right," I said. "Come on."

His bantam car was against the curb in front of the house. I had to jackknife my body to get into it and then my head touched the top. He put it in gear and set it at top speed toward the heart of the city, rushing up to intersections with the horn going, driving as though there were no other cars anywhere.

"Do I frighten you?" he asked as he hesitated for a stop sign, then plunged across.

"I was brought up in Mexico."

"We're all alike," Madero said. "We can't get used to machines. You've seen a charro riding into town. He walks his horse to the edge of the place, then digs his spurs in and charges up to the zocalo. We drive that way. You mentioned a trap. How did you set it?"

"I showed her the paper," I said. "I knew that if she was involved she would pass on the information."

He could have called me a fool again but he didn't. He said "I should have known you would do that. Then I could have had men watching the monastery and the church."

"What made you come?"

"Someone sent me," Madero said.

"Who?"

"Miss Gage."

So Penny's aunt had worried about me, I thought. It was a good warm thought. "She called you?"

"Yes. If she had found me sooner, it would have been a different story, I think. But I was not available for a while. I guessed wrong. I thought you had another plan. I thought you knew who the murderer was and had gone to his home." We missed a cab by inches, slid around a corner into San Juan de Letran and raced south.

"Do you?" I asked.

He evaded the question. He said, "I was confused. I do not blame myself too much. There were two puzzles and the pieces were jumbled. Now they are separate."

I waited for an explanation. It wasn't forthcoming. He turned the car east and stopped it so suddenly near the house where Dorothy Allen lived that I nearly went through the windshield. He was around the car and helping me out while I was getting my legs untangled. We hurried up the steps.

There was a man standing in the entrance hall. The man was John Aldrich.

"Mitchell." He faced us and there was a look of bewilderment on his face. Then his gaze riveted itself on my shoulder and he took a step toward me. "You're hurt, boy. What is it, boy?"

He seemed surprised. He seemed genuinely concerned at the blood on my coat. Was he? I didn't explain. I said, "Miss Allen. Have you seen her?"

"No. I've been ringing her bell. She doesn't answer."

"She may be at the El Toro."

"No. She should be here. She called me and said she would be here."

"Called you? When?" Madero asked.

"Around seven. Seven-thirty."

"Yes?"

"She said she had just seen Mitchell," Aldrich said. "Said he had part of a page from an old book and she thought she knew who had the book."

"Why are you here?"

"At her request."

"She asked you to come?"

Aldrich nodded. He kept his finger on the bell. "Said to stop by between nine and ten. That she might know something of importance then. I came up a minute ago. But she doesn't answer her bell and the entrance door is locked."

Madero had a bunch of keys out and was poking at the lock.

"An odd thing," Aldrich said. "Just as I drove up, someone came out. I thought I recognized him."

"Who?" Madero shoved a key in, turned it.

"I'm not sure. I may be mistaken. I've only seen him a couple of times. But it looked like Ruiz. He ran down the stairs and went west."

The door was open. Madero was inside and we were on his heels hurrying up and along the hall. His knuckles hit the door of her apartment, but he didn't wait. He thrust the key in and turned it and pushed the door open. We looked at darkness. There was a low, steady humming in the room.

His hand fumbled along the jamb and then light filled the place. Dorothy Allen was at home. Her body lay face down on the worn rug near the couch and her blond hair was matted with blood.

TWENTY-TWO

THE LIGHTS seemed to grow dim. I stared at the body and it was as though the room were filled with smoke and I was peering through the smoke at the crumpled form on the floor. There was a chair near me. I dropped into it and then the room was full of light again. I heard the low humming and realized the electric fan was on. I looked at John Aldrich. He was pulling at a fold of skin under his jaw. His face had lost the flush; it was gray. I looked down at his shoes and then let my gaze move slowly up to his shoulders. He wore a brown tweed coat and gray flannel trousers and black shoes. The shoes were dry. I glanced at my own. They were stained with mud and slime and the soles were soaking.

Madero lit a cigarette. The French telephone lay near her body and there was blood on the receiver. He touched it with his toe, pivoted slowly and when he faced the table by the open windows let his gaze rest there. On the table, near my brother's picture, was a bottle of ink and there was a pen and a box of stationery beside it. A straight chair lay on its back near the table. He put his hands in his pockets and went over to the table and stood there letting smoke trickle out his nose.

It was cold in the room. The fan kept turning toward me and pushing a blast of air around me. On the couch there was a blanket bunched in the corner. I shivered.

"Oh my God," Aldrich said.

Madero looked at him. "You think you saw Ruiz leaving the place?"

"I'm not sure. I could be mistaken. It was a man who resembled Ruiz."

"You say she called you between seven and seven-thirty?"

He was staring at my shoes. His glance moved to Aldrich's feet.

"Yes."

"Where were you?"

"At my—" Aldrich was fumbling in his pockets. He didn't finish the sentence until he had put a cigarette between his lips—"office. I had some work to do. I stayed there and finished it. Then I called Mitchell at the hotel but he was out. I tried to get Miss Allen on the phone but the line was busy. So I came here. I thought you would be here, boy."

"You're certain you stayed at the office?"

Aldrich gulped. He took a couple of steps toward the detective. "You don't think—"

Madero cut his speech in two. "That you killed her? No, Mr. Aldrich. I don't think that. I know you didn't kill her."

His sigh was audible above the hum of the fan. He ran his hand across his eyes.

Madero was moving around the room now, peering into drawers, poking into cupboards. In the corner where the gas plate was he pulled the curtain aside and stood looking at it. Then he went back to the body and knelt beside it and stared at her white face.

What Aldrich had told us churned in my mind and wrapped fear all around me. She had called him and mentioned the book and the bit of page torn from the book. That might mean she knew nothing. That might mean she was trying to help. Had she called Ruiz too? And Amaro? In this way to find out who wanted that piece of paper? Another murder on my head then? I found myself looking at the fan, staring at the whirring blades, and then I wondered why it was on. It wasn't hot in the room. It was cold.

"Do something," Aldrich said. "For God's sake, do something, Madero."

Madero straightened. "There's no hurry, Mr. Aldrich."

"But if it was Ruiz—"

"We'll find him," Madero said. "Now I must telephone. You wait here, gentlemen. I won't be long." With that he was gone.

We waited. After a little while the light began to fade again. I saw Aldrich standing in front of me.

"You look like death, Mitchell."

"I feel like it," I said. "Shut the fan off, please."

He crossed the room and the humming stopped. "Lie down a bit, Mitch."

I let him lead me to the couch and somehow it didn't matter that Dorothy Allen's body was so close. I stretched out and he covered me with the blanket and sat on the arm of the couch looking worried. Something was digging into my leg. I pulled it out. He stared at the knife in my hand.

"That killed Joe Briggs," I said. "Madero gave it to me. I found the paper in the handle."

He took it, his hand closed over the hilt. I shut my eyes. "You twist the blade half right and then a quarter back," I said. "The thing comes apart."

"Feel any better?"

"I'm fine," I said. "I was cold. I'm not any more."

"Who shot you, Mitch?"

"It was dark. I couldn't see."

I felt his hand on my forehead. I opened my eyes. He was standing over me and the knife was in his left hand. There was

133

a curious look on his face and there came into my mind a sudden, awful fear. I wanted to get up and wrest the knife from him. I wanted to be out of the room.

He smiled. "Sleep a bit, boy." And moved to the window. I pushed my fear of him away and closed my eyes again.

I must have dozed. There were voices at the door. I sat up and was sorry for it for my shoulder was on fire. Madero came into the room and there was a man in white with a black bag in his hand right behind Madero. And behind the doctor were two policemen and Ruiz was between them, looking frightened. When Ruiz saw Dorothy's body, he stopped and put his hand over his eyes and moaned a little.

"The shoulder," Madero said in Spanish and nodded at me. "Over here," the doctor said. He was a young man with a doleful mouth and very black eyes. I sat in the chair he indicated and he opened my shirt and pulled the crude bandage away.

"A scratch," the doctor said and he seemed unhappy about it. "But it is nothing."

"You should have it," I said. Two other men came in then and they were carrying a basket. I was glad that the doctor was probing the wound because the pain kept me from thinking too much. Then it was over and the men with the basket were gone and the doctor was gone. Another Mexican had come in and he was hunting fingerprints, but Madero paid him no heed. Madero was looking at Ruiz, who was sitting very straight in the chair by the door. Aldrich was still standing by the window, but he didn't have the knife. It lay on the table near Arthur's picture.

"Is this the one?" Madero asked.

Aldrich hesitated. "I'm not sure."

Madero spoke to Ruiz. "When Mr. Aldrich drove up a little while ago he saw a man walking down the steps. He thinks that man was you."

Ruiz was nervous, you could see that. Yet he made no attempt to deny that he was the man Aldrich had seen. He said, "It was."

134

"You were here then?"

"In this room? No."

"Explain, Mr. Ruiz."

"I rang her bell," Ruiz said. The hand that held his half-burned cigarette was shaking. "There was no answer. I rang several times. Then I went away."

"You did not come upstairs?"

"No. Only to the entrance hall. The door was locked."

"And why did you come here?"

"To see Miss Allen, naturally."

Another detective would have been impatient. Not Madero. "But why?"

"To ask her why she was not at the El Toro."

"And your interest, Mr. Ruiz?"

"I own the El Toro," Ruiz said. "Miss Allen works for me." Again he put his hand over his eyes. There were beads of sweat on his temples.

"Miss Allen did not call you?"

"No. I tried to call her but the phone remained busy. So I came."

"You own the El Toro, yet you came rather than send another employee?"

Ruiz took a deep breath. "The others were busy, señor. Tonight the El Toro is crowded."

"When you went away did you see Mr. Aldrich?"

"I saw no one."

"A car. Did you notice a car drive up?"

"I noticed nothing. There may have been one."

"That's all. Thank you," Madero said. He motioned to the policeman. "Take him away. To my office at the Palace." Then he followed them out of the room. He was gone but a moment and when he came back he was smiling blandly. The fingerprint man straightened and dusted his hands. "Finished," he said in Spanish.

"Go then," Madero said. "You too, Mr. Aldrich. That is all."

135

"Do you believe him?" Aldrich demanded sourly. He was pacing nervously in front of the window.

"The case against him is closed," Madero said gently. "Thank you for waiting for me."

"He killed her then?"

Madero shrugged. "He says not."

"Come, John," I said. "You can take me to the hotel."

"But no." Madero took the knife from the table and put it in his breast pocket. "You will come with me, Dr. Drake. The Mexican law is peculiar. You were a witness to the murder of Mr. Brent. There is a matter of a statement."

"Murder." Aldrich put horror in his voice. "Another."

"Yes, another," Madero said. "Come, Dr. Drake."

"All right," I said wearily, and we left the room where Dorothy Allen had died, where my brother's picture still stood on the table with a faded flower in front of it.

When we reached the street, Aldrich asked again about the murder, but Madero waved him away. So he squeezed my good arm and said to call him if I needed anything. Then he got into his car and drove away. Madero stood at the curb watching the tail light disappear. Then he got under the wheel.

"Were you frightened?" he asked, as he put his foot on the starter.

"Frightened? Of what?"

"Of remaining in the room with a murderer," Madero said.

TWENTY-THREE

WE DIDN'T go to the police station. We drove across town to the Horse and I thought of Paul Brent and of the men he had hired to attack me. We went past the Horse and out Reforma Boulevard and turned right in front of the Reforma Hotel and parked the car. I didn't ask questions. I knew that if Madero wanted to explain, he would; that no amount of questioning could make him talk until he was ready. It didn't make sense.

He called Aldrich a murderer, yet let him go. He called Aldrich a murderer, yet said Aldrich had not killed Dorothy Allen. And he kept Ruiz in custody. Too, I was grateful for silence. A great weariness had settled on me, a weariness of body and mind and spirit. What there had been of my world seemed down around my ears—I seemed to have been plunged into a dark pit out of which there was no escape. I knew that in a few moments I would see Penny, and the thought only served to make me the more miserable.

"You are a strange young man," Madero said, as he helped me from the car. "A very strange young man. Foolish and brave. Impetuous yet patient. And so blind. The training perhaps. Equipped to deal with the past but not the present. Why do you not ask the reason for our presence here?"

I spoke in his tongue. "One waits for an explanation."

"There is one who worries about you," Madero said. "That is why we are here. That is one reason."

I was grateful for Molly Gage's interest. It didn't surprise me, for since first we had met she had not tried to hide the fact that she liked and respected me. But it was small recompense. I had seen too much of horror and death in too short a time. John Aldrich's guilt, coming on the heels of all that had happened, filled me with a numb despair. Mechanically I asked, "The other?"

"I did not wish you to go with Mr. Aldrich."

We went up the stairs and the doorman gave us a look of distaste. I didn't blame him. Madero might have found me in the gutter. I remembered seeing a man sleeping beside a pig on the road to San Angel and knew I was more disreputable than he had been. We got in the elevator and the boy cocked an eye at me and grinned. I think he believed I was drunk. I felt drunk. My heart was pounding against my ribs and my legs were weak and my tongue seemed too big for my mouth. I wanted, more than anything, to be alone in darkness. We went along the hall and Madero rapped lightly on the door. It opened and Molly Gage was standing there, concern in her eyes, and Penny was right behind her.

"Mitchell," Molly Gage said. "We were so very worried about you, Mitchell." She took my good hand and held it.

"I need a drink," I said, and it was hard to get the words out.

Penny's face was white and her eyes seemed at the moment much too big. She said faintly, "Are you hurt badly?" I saw pity in her glance. I didn't want pity. I shook my head.

"A scratch," Madero said, casually. "His God took care of him." He didn't say which God, but I knew the one he meant.

There was a brandy bottle on the low table by the couch. And beside the bottle was the chess board where Molly Gage had been working problems. There was a book on chess openings by the board. I stood looking down at it and found myself working out the next move. Then Penny's aunt put a glass in my hand and filled it with brandy. I emptied it.

"Sit down, for God's sake," Molly Gage said. I sat. Penny stood by the table and she seemed to be hunting for words. Nervous and frightened, I thought. I wondered if she had seen Magnin. I wondered if she had discovered that Paul had told her the truth.

"You are full of questions," Madero said, holding his glass to the light. "Do you wish the answers now?"

We didn't speak. We waited. I put the glass on the table and leaned back. I wanted sleep. I wanted sleep and darkness.

Madero opened his cigarette case, put his thumbnail under a cigarette, flipped it, caught it in his mouth and looked pleased with himself. "In Tucson, I learned it," he said. "I have a brother who runs a cinema in Tucson. There was a magician working in the theater. He taught me the trick." He sat down and sipped his brandy. The look in Molly Gage's eyes told me she was seething with impatience. I wasn't. There was no hurry now. Nothing mattered. Arthur was dead and all the others were dead, and knowing wouldn't help. "We wait for a telephne call," Madero added.

"Please," Molly Gage said. "Stop being Charlie Chan."

Madero chuckled. "My wife calls me William Powell. She saw him in *The Thin Man*. I see no resemblance."

I knew Penny was watching me. I looked up and she dropped her glance. She passed in front of me and sat at the other end of the couch. Her hands were in her lap and there was a knotted handkerchief in her fingers.

The little detective threw a smile at me. I knew he wanted an indication of curiosity. I said, "The patience wears thin. Why did you let John Aldrich go if he is a murderer?"

"Aldrich," Molly Gage repeated, and horror made her voice thin.

"The treasury gets empty, my dear doctor," Madero said.

"Stop being cryptic," Molly Gage snapped.

"At the beginning, I start," Madero said. He wouldn't be hurried, I could see that. The situation pleased him. He was the Indian, sitting on a hillside by a fire, and time meant nothing. There was tomorrow and tomorrow. "There is much I do not know," he went on. "There was a book, an old book. It told of something hidden in a tunnel. What? We do not know yet. Soon we will." The mystery of it intrigued him. He lapsed into smiling silence as though savoring each morsel of the strange case.

"Please," Molly Gage said impatiently.

He glanced at her. I knew what he was thinking. An American, he was thinking. No patience. No ability to relish the fine flavor of expectancy. He said, "Dr. Drake's brother found the book some time ago. Perhaps a year. Perhaps longer. He tore from it part of a page and secreted that bit of paper in the handle of a knife."

I was impatient now. I wanted him to be done with it. I wanted to ask about Joe Briggs. I wanted to ask a great many other questions. But I remained silent. I looked at Penny sitting a few feet from me, head bent a little, absorbed apparently in the knotted ball that had been a handkerchief. It ocurred to me that her profile had the fine clearness of a head on a new coin.

"I have not seen the book," Madero went on. "I may not see it. I can only guess. It was written, I suppose, some centuries ago. Mr. Drake pried from it the secret. He rented a house and dug an entrance to the tunnel. Then Mr. Aldrich discovered the secret, too, and killed him and buried him in the tunnel."

Again there was that irritating pause, the little detective sitting there smiling down at the chess board, a smile that had no self-satisfaction in it, but rather a quiet amusement at the ways of men. "I said there were two problems," he continued presently. "I was confused because I did not know that at first. There was the organization known as the Sons of Cortez. The existence of that organization, whose membership is growing far too rapidly for the comfort of my government, came to light last summer. I was assigned to uncover the leaders.

"You think that is a simple task?" He waved his hand. "You underestimate then the strength of the conservatives in this country that gradually fights its way toward the light. Literature attacking the government was flooding Mexico. It was printed, I discovered, in the basement of a house in Guadalajara. An empty house. Next door lived some gentlemen employed by the Bureau of Anthropology, among them Mr. Drake. The press had been made in Chicago. I investigated. I found that the press had been purchased with an American Express money order bearing the signature of Mr. Drake. What was I to do think? Mr. Drake must be questioned. But he had vanished. I started looking for him. You, Doctor, started looking for him. So, ostensibly, did Aldrich. And so did the late Mr. Briggs. Then Mr. Briggs was murdered. Do you blame me for being confused? I hardly blame myself."

His cigarette was out. He put it in an ash tray, put his glass on the table, then hurriedly retrieved it and carefully wiped the base with his handkerchief. "The home training," he observed. "You see I am a family man."

"Yes," said Molly Gage. Penny had turned her head and was looking at me. Our eyes met and the trace of a smile touched her lips. I wanted to speak to her. I wanted to tell her not to pity me, that I didn't need pity.

"I started with a false premise," Madero said. "I worked on the theory that Mr. Briggs had been murdered because of something he had learned in connection with the Sons of Cortez. I was"—he glanced at the table—"playing two chess games on the same board. Until that bit of paper turned up in the knife handle I believed that Mr. Drake, Aldrich, Miss Allen, Amaro, Ruiz and Magnin were all involved in a reactionary revolution."

At the mention of Magnin's name I saw Penny flush and I ached for her. Youth with its disillusions, I thought. At the moment, life must seem very dark.

Madero's voice droned on. "Once I separated the pieces, it was simple. I'll dispose of the Sons of Cortez. The headquarters in the capital is the El Toro. Do you wonder that the blacks and the whites were mixed up? Ruiz is the leader. Amaro his chief strategist. Magnin is a new recruit. That he is connected with the organization is due to Amaro. They had met before. Magnin came here and crossed Amaro's path again. He was introduced to Ruiz, who saw in him a valuable ally—a man with no scruples and a vast knowledge of revolutionary tactics and a fear of death. So Magnin agreed to trade his knowledge for safety. Fair enough, yes?"

"We've had enough of Magnin," Molly Gage said and I was grateful to her.

"Quite," said Madero. "But bear with me a moment. You see, I am apologizing to myself for being inept. So closely were the two matters bound up. Only today I learned that it was Ruiz who used Mr. Drake's name in purchasing that printing press over a year ago, when Mr. Drake was in Vera Cruz doing field work for his bureau." He gave me a little smile. "There, Dr. Drake, was the clue to the murder."

I knew he wanted no comment. I gave him none. He said: "You came here, Dr. Drake, knowing only that your brother was missing. You came because Aldrich sent for you to give you information that was important. That information? A girl had appeared. Miss Allen. A girl who produced a letter showing she was to have married your brother in February, a letter written from Vera Cruz. You assumed, naturally, that the letter—bearing the month, but not the year—was written last December. You assumed that it was this February that your brother and Miss Allen planned to be married."

"Yes," I said. I was talking to myself.

"But Mr. Briggs didn't." Madero repeated the cigarette trick he had learned from the magician in Tucson, and beamed his satisfaction at his skill. "No. He wasn't taken in. With reason. Now this is conjecture. I'm assuming. Apparently, Mr. Briggs knew something of your brother's affairs. Perhaps he saw your brother and Miss Allen together. Perhaps your brother confided in him. He read the letter. He knew Mr. Drake had been in Vera Cruz not last December, but a year ago in December. He knew the Drake-Allen affair was closed. And knowing, he suspected foul play." He said the words with relish. "Foul play," he repeated. "So he questioned Miss Allen. She passed her knowledge of Mr. Briggs' suspicions on to Aldrich. Aldrich removed Mr. Briggs from the scene."

I saw him lying on the couch again. I saw him in the darkening room again and I wanted to cry out. I moved my left shoulder and physical pain was a relief.

"Not conclusive, though," Madero observed. "No proof. One needs proof. Mr. Briggs was dead. But the servants weren't. Mr. Drake's servants, that he didn't hire."

I sighed. Blind, I thought. I should have known enough to question.

"Mr. Drake rented a house on the Street of the Crying Woman," Madero explained. "Rented it for one reason—because it stood above a tunnel and he wanted to enter that tunnel unobserved. He did not know, apparently, where the entrances of that tunnel were. He knew only that it ran beneath a certain house. So he leased the house and dug a pit. Now it occurred to me that a man engaged in digging a pit would have no servants around. I visited the Bureau of Labor, which has admirable records. I discovered that the servants were employed by a man who answered not Mr. Drake's description but the description of Mr. Aldrich, a man who gave his name, however, as Arthur Drake. I questioned the servants. Yes, they had seen Mr. Drake. A man of middle age with a mustache and a red face. A fine gentleman."

"Why?" I asked. "Why, in God's name? Look at the chance he took."

"No chance," said Madero. "Did you describe your brother to them? Of course not. You asked when he had gone and they told you. They were truthful. A man who said he was Arthur Drake put them in the house, said for them to remain until he came back. Did Aldrich go to the house with you? No."

"And when I suggested firing them, he took care of the matter," I said.

"You see," said Madero, "Mr. Aldrich had investigated the tunnel. He had found a simpler way to enter. So he hired the servants and put them in the house. Then no one could disturb him. And he went about his search. But he didn't know where to look. There was the tunnel—half a mile long. He had made a mistake. He had killed Mr. Drake before he learned the whole secret. So he sent for you."

"And searched my room at the Ontario," I said.

"How could he know your brother had confided in no one but the knife?" Madero asked. "He brought you here in the hope you might, unwittingly, have possession of the key. Tonight you gave it to him. Tonight, through Miss Allen, you told him where to go. And he was suspicious. He waited in the dark and you came. He tried to kill you, but fate—" He spread out his hands.

"Not fate," I said.

"The angel-faced one, then," Madero said.

Penny was staring at him and her fingers were touching her lips.

"A brave one," Madero said softly. "A very brave one. He took a bullet meant for another."

Penny moaned. She put her face in her hands.

"A candle burns for him," Madero said. "My wife—" His gesture was expressive. "Life. . . . Who knows why? So Aldrich knew he had been betrayed. And he hurried to Miss Allen's apartment."

"You said he didn't kill her," I put in.

"He didn't," Madero agreed. "She killed herself. She was dead when he arrived. Gas. The fan, Dr. Drake. The blanket on the couch. The open windows."

"No," I said. And my mind asked why.

He seemed to hear the unspoken question. He shrugged. "Why? Remorse. The mind. Who knows what goes on in the mind?"

"But why would a man make a suicide into a murder?" I asked.

"Mr. Aldrich took the answer," Madero said. "The pen and ink, Dr. Drake. A letter was written. From that letter he learned there was no betrayal, perhaps. Or he learned that you were still in ignorance. Remember what Ruiz said? No car he saw. But Aldrich saw Ruiz. Heard the bell when it rang. Saw him from the window. So. Time, he needed. A little more time. He knew—from the letter which I'm sure she wrote— that you were still in the dark. Murder, then. Throw us off the track. Set us on Ruiz. So I oblige. I arrest Ruiz—which had to be done anyway—I let Aldrich go."

"Because the treasury is empty?" Molly Gage said. "Or because you still need proof?"

"I have proof enough." His tone was light as the smoke from his cigarette. "In his car under the seat there was a gray flannel coat. There was slime on the coat. When I left you in the apartment I looked. And a pair of rubbers, still wet. You saw the dry shoes, Dr. Drake. But they were black shoes. One does not wear black shoes and a brown coat."

For the first time Penny spoke. She didn't look up. She

said, "One does if one is Dr. Drake." Her voice was so low I could barely hear it. I looked down at my clothes and I saw Madero looking at them and I thought I saw disapproval in his eyes. But he said nothing. He emptied his glass, moved to the table and started arranging the chess men. Penny's aunt and the little detective were deep in the game when the phone rang. I was sitting there doing a great deal of thinking; I was wondering what was going on in Penny's mind.

TWENTY-FOUR

HE LAY on the floor of the tunnel, 152 paces from the stone with the rude cross above it. There were stones strewn about him and there was a chisel and a hammer close at hand. Above, at the height of a man's shoulder, there was a hole.

Four men squatted against the wall smoking cigarettes and blinking in the light of Madero's flash lamp. One of them had a machine gun in his lap.

"You are efficient," Madero said. "I knew you would be, Jesus."

The man called Jesus said, "It was nothing, my chief, nothing at all."

"Tell me," said Madero.

"We waited," Jesus said. "We saw him go into the monastery to the altar and push the altar aside. Joaquin and I went to the pit. We left Eulalio and Ruben to guard the altar."

"It was bad in the pit," another said. I guessed he was Joaquin. "Very bad," he added. "A dead man not ten feet away."

"And then?" Madero asked.

"He came," Jesus said. "We heard him. Light flashed in the hole. But we were pressed against the wall and he could not see us. We heard him walk away. We heard the pounding of his hammer. Then we crawled into the tunnel. And we crawled along the tunnel."

"I had the flashlight," Joaquin said. "The big one. I turned it on."

Joaquin made a sound like a machine gun. "Finished."

"I am pleased," Madero said. I knew he was thinking of the empty exchequer. I knew he was thinking that there would be no foolish expense for trials and executions. He wasn't being brutal. He was being sensible. He was being an Indian. "Did you examine the hole?"

"Ah, yes," said Joaquin. "But he had not completed the work."

"Complete it, then," Madero said. He bent down and ran his hands through Aldrich's pockets. When he straightened he had a letter. He held it in the light of his flash. "For you." He put it in my hand.

I found a comparatively dry place near the wall, sat down and held my flashlight between my knees and put the letter in the beam. Across the tunnel Joaquin was banging away at the chisel, loosening the mortar between the stones. And as I read what Dorothy Allen had written before she died, I wondered if what lay behind that wall was worth the price it had cost.

My dear, my very dear Mitchell,

I told you I had found out what love is and you said you knew, but you didn't know. I told you when you love someone, not to lose them. I won't lose you. I take the memory of you with me, the memory of your dear thin face and your wild hair and your eyes, so bright your eyes, and so blind. Such a strange ending. But there can be no other. And it is an unhappy one only because of what I have to tell you. Could I say only, Mitchell, I adore you, then it would be fine and very sweet. But there is more than that to say.

I said I was hard. Take that as an explanation, Mitchell. I came up the hard way, the bitter way. And two years ago I met Arthur and I was still hard.

I never loved him. He thought he loved me. Then he found out things about me and was through. We were to have been married last year but in Vera Cruz he met a man and the man talked out of turn. Was it true, he asked me. And I said yes, and that was the end.

I didn't care. I didn't have it in me to care about anything then. There were other men. And there was always John Aldrich. He's been mixed in my life for years. It was through him I met Arthur. We're alike, John and I. No scruples. Nor morals. I won't go into that.

I lied to you about the book as I've lied about many things. (Only one lie I'm sorry for—the flower in front of his picture. That was a cheap lie, Mitchell darling.) I saw that book. Arthur found it a year and a half ago in a ruin near Guadalajara. It was written by a monk—Brother Hipolito—in the fifteen hundreds. You'll never see it. John destroyed it after he murdered Arthur.

It was, Brother Hipolito said, his confession. The story of his life. Most of it had nothing to do with the treasure, so I'll skip it. It's the treasure that is important—or we thought it was. I know better now. Anyway, Brother Hipolito told of supervising the building of a tunnel from his monastery to a church and of uncovering a number of gold ingots. Two other monks were with him and they swore each other to secrecy, put the treasure in a chest and put the chest in a hole they made in the tunnel wall. Then Brother Hipolito sinned. He called it a most grievous sin, I remember. He killed his brother monks. But he was punished for it, he said. By God, he said. He went blind. So he wrote his story and Arthur found it. Found it hidden in a rusty old box under the altar of a church he was reconstructing.

Brother Hipolito wasn't entirely honest in his confession. He didn't say where the tunnel was. Just said it was between a monastery and a church somewhere. Arthur started looking for it.

How he traced Brother Hipolito to Mexico City I don't know exactly. He said once he had a hunch it was Mexico City. He said that in the flight of the Spaniards from the Aztecs there was a good deal of treasure dropped in the canals of Tenochitlan. Also, he found out Brother Hipolito was a Benedictine. I always considered that a drink, didn't you?

We broke up and I started seeing John again and one night when I was tight I told John about the book. He started on Arthur's trail and from then on I stayed out of the picture. It wouldn't have done to let Arthur know John and I were thick again. Arthur was wise. He held his tongue. But when he leased that house he made a mistake. He had John draw up the lease and John guessed what he was up to. He did some spying, saw Arthur digging, and waited.

John didn't intend to murder Arthur, I know that. With all his faults he was fond of Arthur. But he wanted money—needed it badly. Most of his property had been expropriated and he was bitter about it, bitter against the Mexican government and against the world in general. One night when he thought Arthur was away he sneaked into the tunnel. Arthur wasn't away. Arthur caught him and they fought in the dark and he killed Arthur. He didn't tell me about it. I guessed it, finally, and asked him. Then he said it was an accident. That Arthur had fallen and hit his head.

John searched that tunnel from one end to the other, but it was no use. The page that said where it was hidden was torn from the book. Then he decided you might have the page, so he sent for you. You came and John had to have an excuse, so he showed you the letter Arthur had written when we were engaged, and you accepted it. But Joe Briggs didn't. He saw me that afternoon and asked for the truth. I called John, and John went to his apartment and waited, and when he came in he murdered him.

I would have gone on with it. If you hadn't been you, I would have gone on with it. But I knew tonight I was through with living. Blind boy. So apparent in your scheming. I knew, darling. I knew so well what you were up to. So I played your game for you, knowing you and Madero would be waiting in the tunnel when John came.

He must be dead now. **I feel no** guilt at the betrayal. If it had profited him to let me **down, he would** not have hesitated.

Oh, my dear, my very dear. **Be** happy, darling. Be very happy. And sometimes remember

Your Dorothy

I folded the letter and put it in my pocket. This was the end then. Five centuries ago Brother Hipolito had come this dark way to leave a heritage of death. I looked across the tunnel.

They were pulling the stones out and dropping them. They reached into the hole with eager hands and close by Madero was standing, an unlit cigarette between his lips and his hands in his pockets.

There was the scrape of metal against stone. Joaquin shouted and his shout echoed through the passageway. Six pair of hands reached up and lifted it down and as I looked at the rusty iron chest, I shuddered. Seven. The blood of seven on it.

Jesus tugged at the lid. It didn't give. He hit it with the hammer, pounding it loose and the rust flaked off and fell on the slimy stones. Then it was open.

I moved close and peered inside. Brother Hipolito's treasure was a pile of stones. Someone had been before us. Someone had learned the monk's secret long ago.

TWENTY-FIVE

WE ATE dinner in the patio a few nights later. My brother lay in the cemetery with Mother and Father. The pit was filled in and the tunnel was left to its ghosts. It was a farewell dinner, for Molly Gage and Penny and I were going home next day.

There was chicken with a rich brown sauce and tacos and peppers in a golden crust. And there was a strange dessert made of avocados—or aguacates, as Madero called them. There were candles on the table and after a while the full moon peered over the wall.

Madero's two fat little daughters, Dolores and Juanita, sat at the table. The Señora had protested but Madero was firm.

"We are moderns," he said.

"In the better families children eat alone," the Señora said.

"Spanish families, not Mexican," Madero said. He laughed. Then he translated for Molly Gage's benefit.

It was a warm night, full of silver and magic. Penny was there across from me, and Molly Gage was beside me. We didn't talk of murder. It wasn't easy not to.

But we closed that chapter of our lives as best we could.

Madero did much of the talking. He told us about his childhood in the mountains. He had been a muleteer for a while and every now and then he longed for the old life. Then he had worked in the silver mines at Pachuca and later had been a coffin maker's helper in San Angel. That was when he was going to school. A good life, he said. A full life. Now he was content as man could be. No man was entirely content, ever.

He was dressed for the occasion in one of his innumerable gabardine suits and his hair was almost as polished as his shoes. But he didn't seem comfortable. With all his talk about the new Mexico, I sensed a yearning in him for the old life—for pajamas and serapes and huaraches, for the charcoal makers' fires on the hillsides, for the mitla and the hill roads.

We had brandy there under the night sky. It was Mexican brandy, with a sharp bite to it. I liked it. I had always liked it. It, too, was Mexico. Then Madero glanced up at the moon. He said, "There will be many in the gardens tonght." He spoke to his wife in Spanish. He said, "Remember. The music and the moon and the singing."

"And the beer," Señora Madero said. "Always the beer."

"One cannot make love without beer," Madero said. He fished in his pocket and brought out a card. He said in English, "My brother operates several boats at Xochomilco. Some day you may go, eh?"

"Thanks," I said, and took the card.

"For nothing," Madero said. "What do you do when you return to the United States?"

"Teach," I said. "And write."

"A good life, too," Madero said. "And you, Miss Gage?"

"I don't know," Penny said.

The children were nodding. The Señora bustled off with them, made them stop in the doorway and call good night to us. And when she came back we got up to go.

"You will come again?" the Señora asked.

Molly Gage smiled and squeezed her hand. Without knowing Spanish, she understood. One didn't need a translator when Señora Madero smiled.

"Mitchell," Penny's aunt said. "Tell her to visit us. Tell her they will always be welcome." I told her. Then we were outside and Madero was in the doorway bobbing his head.

"My brother," he said. "Watch him. He is a sharp one. Don't pay more than four pesos an hour. He will ask twelve, without the card. With the card, he will ask eight. But pay only four." The door closed. That was the last I ever saw of José Manuel Madero. And now the door between us was shut and our lives were separate again, I knew how much I liked and respected the little man.

"I'm tired," Molly Gage sighed.

"I'll take you home," I said.

"The moon is full," Penny said. "Remember?"

"Yes?"

"At Chapultepec," Penny said. "You said some day when the moon was full we would go to Xochomilco. It's full tonight."

We got a taxi. Penny sat in the middle and when her aunt got out at the Reforma, Penny didn't move. We crossed town and turned south and then we were in open country, and up on the hills we could see the little fires of the charcoal makers. We turned east and ahead were the two great mountains sleeping in the night.

We sat close together but we didn't speak for a long time.

There was a great deal to say but where was one to begin? I didn't know. So I sat there and watched the moon-drenched fields slip by and then we were at the canal and a horde of Mexicans surrounded us. I produced the card. A man even shorter than Madero pushed up to me and beamed. Friends of his brother? A great man, his brother. A valuable man to Mexico. Had I heard how he solved the mysteries of the Street of the Crying Woman? Such detective work! A boat? Eight pesos, señor.

"Four," I said.

"Six," Madero's brother said. There was a union. Did I not believe in unions?

"Four," I said.

He shrugged. "Four, then." But the Señor wished music, certainly.

"Certainly," I said.

That would be four pesos more. Cheap. A ridiculous price really.

"All right," I said.

"Because you are my brother's friend, I do this," he said. "And because the Señorita is lovely."

The moon climbed above the poplars and the canals were strips of silver. We lay in the back of the boat and looked up through the walls of trees. A family party drifted past and there was the smell of food and there was much singing and laughter.

"What did he say?" Penny asked. "He spoke so very fast."

"He said you were lovely," I said.

"What else?"

"He said your eyes were like the corn flowers in his garden," I said.

Our musicians moved up. There were four of them, three guitars and a home-made marimba. They began to play very softly and to sing. They sang *La Paloma,* but I didn't mind. I decided it wasn't such a bad song, really.

"Mitchell," Penny said. "I've been a fool."

"No, Penny."

"I think I've grown up, Mitchell."

"Don't grow up," I said.

"I won't grow up too much," Penny said. "I'll still put people on pedestals."

"Only the right people."

"Only you," Penny said. "He didn't say that, did he? The man at the landing. About the corn flowers. You said it, Mitchell." Her face shut out the moon.

* * *

Some day I'll go back to Mexico again. I'll take the long straight road south from Laredo, down through the jungle to Tamazanchale, then up and over the hills to the broad valley where the maguey plants march across the plain in gray-green rows. Off to the left I'll see the white woman sleeping in the mist, and beyond, the white cone of the smoking mountain. There will be organ cactus sheltering the little huts. There will be men and women and children trudging along the roads carrying their incredible loads. There will be dust and sun and wind, and in a field, a herd of white goats grazing.

This Bantam book contains the complete text of the original edition. Not one word has been changed or omitted. The low-priced Bantam edition is made possible by the large sale and effective promotion of the original edition, published by William Morrow and Company, Inc., under the title *The Street of the Crying Woman*.

FOR YOUR NEXT MYSTERY THRILL:

Angela Pewsey collected lives...
...other people's lives.

She gathered them up in bits and snatches, from scraps of conversation, from stolen letters and spying moments.

Who feared Angela Pewsey?

Every man and woman in the peaceful little village who had the smallest secret to hide.

Who hated Angela Pewsey?

Every villager who got one of her gloating, threatening poisoned letters, everyone whose secret she had discovered.

Who killed Angela Pewsey?
WHO WOULDN'T?

The Voice of the Corpse
BY MAX MURRAY
wherever Bantam Books are sold